The Single Dad
Finds a Wife

Felicia Mason

HARLEQUIN® LOVE INSPIRED®

Recycling programs for this product may not exist in your area.

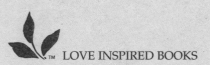

LOVE INSPIRED BOOKS

ISBN-13: 978-0-373-81836-5

The Single Dad Finds a Wife

Copyright © 2015 by Felicia Mason

www.Harlequin.com

Printed in U.S.A.

Love must be sincere. Hate what is evil;
cling to what is good.
—*Romans* 12:9

Love is patient, love is kind.
—*1 Corinthians* 13:4

Acknowledgments

Thank you to Denise P. Jeffries, RN,
for providing medical and clinical information
for this novel. Any mistakes here are mine.

Chapter One

The last thing on David Camden's mind was romance. He had enough complications in his life already without adding the type that generally accompanied females, especially ones his best friend tried to set him up with.

More importantly, he had no babysitter. And he couldn't very well show up at the biggest meeting of his career with a cranky four-year-old in tow.

He had been keeping tabs on the atmosphere in town and reading the articles about the opposition to his project. The online edition of the *Cedar Springs Gazette* carried full coverage, including a slew of testy letters to the editor questioning the need, efficacy and motivation for the project. It was frustrating to know he was walking into Cedar Springs, North Carolina, at a decided disadvantage—before he could even present his ideas for a new mixed-use development.

Historical societies and their hysterical members were the bane of his existence.

"Daddy, my stomach hurts."

David looked up from the open laptop on the desk. Jeremy sat on the pullout sofa in the hotel room they were calling home for the next few days. He closed the email from his best friend; the missive spouted the attributes of someone named Susan that she wanted him to go on a blind date with. As if he had time to date. He was a single dad with a floundering business to run.

"Hey, buddy," he said, rolling the desk chair over to the sofa. "What's this about a tummy ache?"

David crouched before his son. He pressed his hand to the boy's forehead and frowned.

Jeremy had a fever.

Guilt flashed through David. His son hadn't been cranky because he was four. Jeremy had been irritable and out of sorts because he was sick.

David wiped a hand over his face and weighed his options. They were few. A sick kid and important business meetings coming up.

He sighed. It was moments like this that he really missed having the support of a wife.

He didn't know any doctors here in Cedar

Springs, let alone where he might find one at this time of the night. It was already after seven, probably closer to eight. He'd lost track of time with emails and reading the online newspaper.

So he did what anyone else in his situation might do: he called the front desk and asked for recommendations.

Dr. Spring Darling was looking forward to tonight. The Magnolia Supper Club's dinner meetings were always a highlight after a busy workday. And following the stress of this week, she needed the therapy of a relaxing evening with good friends and stimulating conversation that had nothing to do with work. They'd probably review the latest data they'd each gleaned about the mayor's proposed boondoggle—a condo development and shopping center—as if the city needed more of either.

She logged her notes from the last patient and was heading toward the volunteer lounge at the Common Ground Free Clinic and Health Center when a ruckus at the front receptionist's desk caught her attention.

"I'm sorry, sir. We're closed for the evening. The emergency room at Cedar Springs General can—"

"You don't understand," he said. "I...I can't go

to the hospital. I was told to come here. Please, is there a doctor who can see him?"

The clinic's hours made no difference to Spring when a patient was in need. She quickly made her way back to the front, where Shelby Peters was trying to send a man on his way.

The man was holding a small boy in his arms and pleading with the free clinic's by-the-book receptionist.

"What seems to be the problem?" Spring said, stepping forward.

The man's gaze connected with hers, and Spring felt as if a bolt of lightning had hit her. She knew there were people who claimed to know on first sight that someone was The One. Spring had always been the practical Darling sister and didn't believe in such nonsense. Getting to know someone over time, discovering mutual interests, shared values and overall compatibility—those were the qualities that mattered, the elements that determined if a relationship had a chance at being successful. But this was different, and her breath caught from just one look at the man.

The feminine side of her noted his dark eyes, sandy hair and the way he held the boy. She sensed in him a quiet compassion and strength, something that appealed to her on a visceral level. Spring wondered at her reaction to the man as she registered the flushed look of the boy's face. Tamping down thoughts of relationships and the appeal of a dark-eyed stranger, the clinician in her was already running through the paces, assessing the child's demeanor.

"Dr. Darling, you can't keep doing this," Shelby said. "The clinic is not a twenty-four-hour operation."

"Maybe it should be," Spring said. Then to the man holding the boy, she said, "I'm Dr. Darling. Follow me."

"Exam room five is prepped," Shelby said, resignation in her voice.

Spring led the way to the examination room. As they went down the hall, she asked, "What are his symptoms?"

"He was complaining about a stomachache earlier," he said. He put his precious load on the white-paper-covered examination table in the room. "I thought it was too many jelly beans. We got them free at a shop downtown."

Spring nodded. "Sweetings," she said as she went to a small sink, washed her hands and then slipped on a pair of examination gloves. "They give kids free samples."

"The lady must have felt sorry for him—or us," the man told her. "She filled a big bag and gave them to Jeremy. I didn't think he'd eaten that many."

Spring checked the boy's vitals.

"He has a temperature," he continued. "I don't have a thermometer, so I don't know how high, but…"

"It's a low-grade fever," Spring confirmed a moment later. "You said his name is Jeremy?"

The man nodded, his gaze boring into Spring's. She felt as if she'd been overcome with a fever herself. She found it disconcerting but, oddly, not unpleasant.

Shaking off the sensation, she told herself it was compassion, not attraction. The people who came to the Common Ground Free Clinic often had no other available recourse for health care. While her specialty was pediatrics, she, like all the other volunteer physicians, nurses and physician assistants, practiced general medicine here, doing what she could for the patients on-site and making referrals as warranted. Often the clinic picked up the tab for those specialty referrals.

The free clinic's clients were typically the unemployed or underemployed, the working poor who had low-wage jobs with no or inadequate benefits. And then there were the homeless, an ever-growing population in the city of Cedar Springs.

She wondered which category the man and the boy fell into.

He'd said he couldn't go to the hospital. And

then there was the overly generous handout at the downtown bakery and sweetshop. Spring could make a fairly educated guess about their financial situation.

She sent the man a reassuring smile, then gave her full attention to her young patient. "Jeremy, sweetie, does it hurt anywhere?"

He let out a moan in response.

The man winced, a reaction that didn't escape her. He hovered near the top of the table and put his hand on the boy's shoulder.

"My stomach hurts," came a small voice.

"Well, I'm Dr. Spring, and I'm going to see about that, okay?"

Jeremy nodded.

She gave him a cursory exam, feeling along his abdomen and chest, watching his reaction as she pressed or prodded.

The boy moaned again.

"Is he going to be okay?" The father's concern and fear compelled Spring to reassure him in some way, even though she knew she couldn't give him the blanket promise she knew he wanted to hear.

"May I see you for a moment?" she asked him.

He glanced at his son and then nodded. "I'm going to be right over here, buddy. You hang in there—the doctor's going to make it better."

They took a few steps away, just far enough that the child couldn't overhear.

"I'm going to run a few tests," Spring told him. "Just to be on the safe side. It could be a simple tummy ache, but I don't want to rule out anything else unless I'm sure."

"Do you know how much—" the man began.

Spring interrupted. "You don't have to worry about the cost. Our focus here at Common Ground is wellness and health."

"I can pay," he said.

She touched his arm. "It's all right. Really."

A little moan from the examination table drew Spring's attention back to her young patient.

"Everything will be fine," she assured the boy's father.

David didn't know what was more distressing, Jeremy getting sick while they were out of town or this gorgeous doctor thinking he was some kind of deadbeat who couldn't pay for his kid's health-care needs.

And gorgeous she was. Her blond hair, like spun gold sprinkled with shards of sunlight and honey, was pulled up on the sides and clasped with a large barrette to keep it out of her face. She wore simple gold hoops in her ears. Khaki slacks and a crisp white shirt were visible under the unbuttoned white lab coat she had over her clothing.

But something about that name rang a bell with him. What had the receptionist said?

And then he remembered. *Darling.*

Someone named Darling was leading the opposition to his development project.

Great.

Just great, David thought. *What else can go wrong?*

"I think it's a case of gastroenteritis," the pretty doctor said.

David groaned. That sounded serious.

"That sounds…it sounds bad," he said. "Are you sure? Is he going to be okay?"

Dr. Darling smiled and placed a reassuring hand on his arm. Again.

"It sounds much worse than it is," she said. "Gastroenteritis is what most people call the stomach flu. Has he had any—"

"Daddy, I have to go to the bathroom."

"—diarrhea or vomiting?" Spring said at the same time.

David's eyes widened as he looked between the boy and the pretty doctor. She pointed toward the door.

"Second door on the right," she told him.

David scooped up his son and dashed for the rest room.

Twenty minutes later and with his son's diagnosis confirmed, David got instructions from the doctor on what needed to be done.

"He'll need rest and plenty of fluids for the next few days," Spring said. "It's really easy for the little ones to get dehydrated with this sort of illness. He needs plenty of juice, tea or Gatorade. I'm going to give you a prescription. It's an oral electrolyte replacement. Gatorade has some, but this will ensure that he gets all the fluids and minerals he needs. He may not want much to eat, but be sure you give this to him with food, even if it's just a bit of banana or some peanut butter. The protein will do him good. But be sure he starts with soft foods."

"Dr. Darling, I'm not sure—"

"It's already taken care of, Mr.—I'm sorry. I didn't get your name."

"Camden," he said. "David Camden." Then, wondering, he added, "What's already taken care of?"

"The prescription. All you have to do is take this to any pharmacy in town. Common Ground will see to the payment. You just need to make sure Jeremy takes all of the medication, even when he's feeling better."

Her cheery explanation grated on David. Here he was in Cedar Springs to help develop its economic vitality and all she could see was a loser who needed handouts. That Carolina Land

Associates, and thus David Camden himself, was one contract away from just that stung his psyche like salt in an open wound.

For every degree of warmth in her voice, David's dropped until ice chips formed on his words.

"I am not a charity case, Dr. Darling."

Chapter Two

"I didn't presume that you were, Mr. Camden," she said.

If she was upset or insulted by his tone, it didn't show.

David had to give her credit. She didn't snap at him even though he probably deserved it. She spoke the words slowly and evenly. But he did notice an ever-so-slight tightening at the corner of her mouth. If he hadn't been looking directly at said mouth, he would have missed it.

The irrational part of him felt inordinately pleased. He had managed to ruffle her too-cool feathers and the calm-seas demeanor she wore with the ease she wore that white lab coat with the Common Ground logo and her name—*Dr. Darling*—embroidered inside a blue oval.

The rational part of him wanted to tell her that he was worried about his kid. He was worried about his own mother, who was also Jeremy's regular babysitter. The day he'd left for this business trip, she'd taken off for Greensboro, saying she needed to "get away for a few days."

He was worried about his company and the employees who depended on him to secure the deal with the City of Cedar Springs. And, most of all, he was worried that he would fail every last one of them, including and most especially his son.

And to put a cherry on top of the mess of a melted sundae that was his life, it hadn't escaped his notice that she had—again—cut him off and was in fact presuming he couldn't afford to pay.

Was she trying to save him embarrassment?

If that were the case, she did so with a grace and style he could only admire, displaying empathy in a gentle and subtle manner. David had to admit that the line about the peanut butter and banana was smoothly delivered. There was no judgment, no condemnation in her voice, just a statement of fact. He supposed many of her patients here subsisted on peanut butter and bananas, two relatively inexpensive foods that were readily available and nutritious.

After another trip to the little boys' room, Jeremy sat comfortably—at least for the time being—ensconced in a chair that looked like the command station of a galactic battleship or maybe the mission control room for NASA astronauts. He was fighting hard to stay awake to watch a *Sesame Street* video, but David knew sleep would win the skirmish with the four-year-old. On top of being ill, it was way past his usual bedtime.

"Clever way to get the kids comfortable while sick," he said, nodding toward the room where the receptionist had directed him after he'd seen to Jeremy in the restroom.

The doctor smiled, and David knew she'd accepted the olive branch he'd extended by way of a compliment. And he liked the way that smile lit up her face.

"Decorating the children's waiting rooms in themes they could relate to was actually a suggestion of one of our young patients," she said, gesturing toward the all-boy space decorated in blues, blacks and silver. Her blue eyes sparkled, and she gave him a grin that transformed her face. "He didn't care much for the very pink Barbie Dreamhouse that was in a corner and wanted to know why we liked girls more than boys."

David smiled. "Out of the mouths of babes comes genius and inspiration?"

Spring nodded. "Something like that. Then, before you know it, backed by an anonymous gift to the clinic, there was funding to update and remodel not only two kids' waiting-slash-recovery rooms, but also all of the common spaces here. Common Ground was very blessed by that donor.

"But back to Jeremy's care and recovery," she said.

And just that fast she morphed into the cool and efficient physician. David wondered if she had a husband and children who after clinic hours got to see the unmasked Dr. Darling. Her genuine smile seemed like good medicine to him.

"Here you go," the receptionist said, bustling into the waiting room toting a small canvas bag. "How's our patient?"

"Dozing at the moment," Spring said, accepting the bag the woman handed her.

"Everything else is all ready," the receptionist told the doctor. "You just swing by my desk when you're all done. My name's Shelby," she added to David.

"Yes, I will. Thank you," he mumbled. Then, eyeing the bag, which he noted also sported the oval Common Ground logo, he asked Spring, "What everything else?"

"Just the file. Jeremy's charts. She's gotten everything logged in to our medical and service records system. When you return, all you'll need to do is check in. You'll only need to fill out paperwork once. And that's for any Common

Ground ministry. The medical records are, of course, only accessible to staff here at the clinic."

"What exactly is Common Ground?"

"A perfect segue," she said, smiling as she reached into the tote bag the receptionist had handed off to her. She pulled out a brochure and offered it to him.

"This will tell you more about the ministries," she said. "We're a nonprofit partnership run by three churches here in Cedar Springs. In addition to joint community service programs, Common Ground operates a soup kitchen, homeless shelter, this medical clinic and a recreation program. Once you're registered for one service, you're registered for all. One-stop shopping makes it easier for everyone, clients and our volunteers."

David glanced around the waiting room. "So, this is basically a free clinic?"

That telltale tightness appeared at her mouth again, probably prompted by the frustration he had been unable to shield from his voice. What he'd suspected was true. She thought he was a freeloader looking for a handout. He didn't know why that irked him so much. It just did.

He also got the distinct impression she was going to say something, but then the moment passed and she gave him a hospitable smile— not one of the genuine ones she'd bestowed on Jeremy, but that I'm-being-polite-because-I'm-supposed-to smile that Southern girls seemed to perfect in kindergarten, if not as early as in the womb.

"There are sliding rates, Mr. Camden. Shelby will be able to answer any questions you may have, and if she can't, our administrator is available from nine until noon on weekdays."

Contrite now and attributing his earlier bad attitude to stress, David ran a hand through his hair.

She was just doing her job. He didn't need to take his frustrations or his insecurities out on her.

"I'm sorry, Doctor. I…I've had a lot on me these last few months. Jeremy getting sick must have just capped it all. I hope you'll forgive that evil twin who was impersonating me a few moments ago."

She regarded him with what could best be described as wary interest, the kind reserved for the occasion when you run across an injured animal—one that might also have rabies. Then, like sunrise after a night of storms, she smiled and patted him on the arm. He liked when she touched him, even though the touches were nothing more than human kindness, the type that typically went along with what was referred to as a doctor's bedside manner.

"I'm going to check on Jeremy one last time before you go."

He watched her cross the room and then bend toward his son. The shopping bag, he noticed, she'd left on the floor at his feet. He also noticed that she hadn't accepted—or outright rejected—his apology.

As Spring tended to Jeremy she thought about his father.

She wasn't at all sure what to make of her reaction to the man. Not to mention the little sparring match they'd engaged in. She'd sensed hostility in him, quickly followed by what she could only describe as regret.

What was that all about?

With his sandy hair and those worried brown eyes, he was attractive enough—if you went for that type. The type who listened with his whole being, whose gaze seemed to search for hidden and deeper meanings with every glance.

And do you go for that type?

She ignored the taunt of the inner Spring.

"Are you my mom?"

The small voice floated up to her in an awe-filled whisper.

She smiled at the question from her small patient.

"No, Jeremy. I'm Dr. Spring. Do you remember me?"

The boy nodded.

"How's that tummy feeling?"

He made a face. "Where's my daddy?"

"He's right—"

"Hey, buddy," the man said, making Spring start. She hadn't heard him approach. She edged out of the way to give him room, moving to the other side of the big chair. She watched as he ruffled the boy's hair. "I'm right here, Jeremy."

"I wanna go home, Daddy."

He looked over to see what she had to say about that. "Is he all clear?"

Spring nodded.

"I wanna go to our real house," Jeremy added. "Not the hotel."

Spring bit her lip. Her heart ached for them. This father and son needed help, the kind that Common Ground offered, but the man bristled each time she tried to assure him that it wasn't a handout but a help up that the ministry provided.

She had had the training offered to every volunteer and knew she couldn't foist assistance on them. She was on the board of directors and had been one of the people who'd insisted that sensitivity training be a requirement of all Common Ground volunteers. People wanted and needed to maintain their dignity, especially when they found themselves in critical situations.

"You'll be feeling like your normal self in a few days, Jeremy," she told the boy. "Your father is going to give you some medicine to take. Will you promise me you'll be a good trouper and take it?"

The boy nodded.

"Good," she said, smiling at him. She reached into her pocket and pulled out a pen and a small card. She scribbled something on the back and handed it to the boy. "If your tummy hurts again, have your dad call me at this number." Spring patted Jeremy's leg and then glanced up at his father. "Have a good evening, Mr. Camden."

Spring left them then, but she overheard the child's question. "Daddy, is she a spring angel?"

Her smile was wry as she made her way to the physicians' office.

It took her just a few minutes to log her new patient notes, shed her lab coat, pack up her bag and grab her keys. Shelby would be ready to go, as well, as soon as Mr. Camden and his son checked out.

"There has to be some mistake," she heard the man say a few minutes later as she reached the front reception area. "I must have left my wallet at the hotel. I do have insurance."

She started to turn and go out the back way, but the boy, in his father's arm and peering over his shoulder, had seen her.

"Dr. Spring."

She waved at him. Uncertain about how Mr.

Camden might take her overhearing his financial problems, Spring hastened toward the door.

"Mr. Camden, don't worry about it. Really. We don't need an insurance card or payment," Shelby said. "All you have to do is take this to the pharmacy. They'll fill it no questions asked. Here are the directions to an all-night drugstore."

"But…"

Spring's heart broke for them. She'd heard plenty of hard-luck stories in her time volunteering with Common Ground. She had also learned that she couldn't make people's problems disappear the way she could with an illness. A bandage, shot or lollipop could not and did not solve the troubles the clinic's patients faced once they left Common Ground.

Not able to bear hearing any more, she hurried out the doors toward her car.

They obviously needed help, and she was glad she'd used the ploy of giving the Common Ground business card to the child. Handing it to a child patient eased any potential embarrassment of the parent while still getting the necessary contact information into the parent's hands.

Because in addition to a toll-free after-hours clinic number, the contact numbers for both the soup kitchen and homeless shelter were on there. She hoped Mr. Camden wouldn't be too proud to seek the assistance he obviously needed.

She sat in her car for a moment, tears inexplicably welling in her eyes.

She had been blessed with so much. And there were people like Mr. Camden and Jeremy who were just struggling to make it. The *News & Observer*, the daily newspaper out of Raleigh and Durham, was filled with stories about families who'd lost everything in the recession, who were victims of layoffs or downsizing. Of others forced into foreclosures or short sales on their homes. She wondered again what category the Camdens fell in, what had happened to them that put their stability in jeopardy.

I wanna go to our real house.

"Not a hotel," Spring said, sadness seeping into her bones.

She started the car, a sensible and dependable late-model Volvo.

At least Jeremy had a hotel room to sleep in, she thought. That meant they weren't living in a car like so many of the region's homeless population were.

Suddenly not feeling much like an indulgent six-or seven-course gourmet dinner with her friends, Spring pressed a button on her dash panel and told the car phone system to "Call Cecelia."

She'd cancel on the Magnolia Supper Club

tonight and just go home. A bowl of soup, some tea and a good book would suit her just fine.

As she drove out of the parking lot, she glanced in the rearview mirror and saw Mr. Camden emerge from the clinic holding Jeremy in one arm, the Common Ground Free Clinic tote in the other.

Seeing that made her feel a little better.

Shelby had somehow gotten him to take the bag of supplies, samples, coupons and information that every new client received.

The car's remote phone system connected. "This is Cecelia Jeffries," a husky voice said.

"Hey there, Cecelia. It's Spring."

"Oh, for goodness' sakes," her friend said. "You're calling from that car phone again. I didn't recognize the number and thought one of my students had somehow gotten my personal cell. What's up, girl?"

Spring smiled, her friend's voice lifting her spirits. "I'm going to have to cancel on the supper club tonight."

"Cancel? It's already canceled. Didn't you get the messages?"

"Messages? No, I've been at the clinic. We had a late walk-in."

"There was a break-in at the store. Gerald is falling apart."

"Is he okay?" Spring asked, alarmed. Gerald

Murphy did not do well with deviations from the norm. "I can head over there right now." Spring turned toward Main Street instead of the street that would lead to her house across town.

"He's fine," Cecelia said. "You know how he is. Richard has been dealing with the police."

Spring made the left onto Main Street and the downtown district where Step Back in Time Antiques was located.

"I see the police squad car in front of the store," she reported.

"Come over when you leave there," Cecelia said. "I'm making a quick chicken potpie, so at least you'll have a hot meal since you probably just had a protein bar for lunch."

Spring chuckled. "You know me too well."

"Girl, forget saving calories. Life was meant to enjoy—and that means enjoying good food."

"Everything in moderation," Spring said.

Cecelia snorted at that.

After promising that she would stop by after checking on Gerald and Richard, Spring disconnected the call and pulled into a spot on the street behind the Cedar Springs Police Department cruiser.

As she got out of the car and headed toward the door of the shop, a train display in the window of Step Back in Time Antiques caught her eye. She wondered if Jeremy Camden liked trains. She realized that if Mr. Camden was living with his young son in one of the city's low cost extended-stay hotels populated by some of the homeless, the last thing that would be on his mind would be splurging on an antique train set, no matter how fetching.

She couldn't help the sadness she felt knowing that Jeremy wouldn't—*couldn't*—have something as simple as a train set.

Chapter Three

The only thing on David Camden's mind was picking up that prescription, getting Jeremy settled in bed and then figuring out a way to show Dr. Spring Darling that he wasn't the sort who took an unneeded handout. She had to have overheard that fiasco at the front desk.

After that, he would figure out how he was going to make the meetings in the morning with first the public safety officials and then the mayor and planning officials. That his priorities were turned topsy-turvy didn't at all surprise him the way it should have. His son and securing the deal with the City of Cedar Springs should have been his only two concerns. Yet here he was disturbed and wondering about the impression he'd made on a woman he'd just met.

He'd seen her as a woman, someone he could

be interested in and that hadn't happened in a long time.

"Focus, Camden," he coached himself.

He had work to do and none of it involved a tall blue-eyed blonde.

David forced his attention to his current dilemma.

He couldn't take Jeremy with him to the meetings, and he couldn't afford to blow this deal. The opportunity for his company, Carolina Land Associates, was too great, and, in a way, Jeremy's future depended on his sealing the contract.

He also wondered if Dr. Spring Darling was the Darling he'd read about in the online edition of the *Cedar Springs Gazette*—the Darling so vocally opposed to and leading the effort to squelch the very notion of development in the city. But before he could investigate any of that, he needed to make sure Jeremy was all right. A glance over his shoulder and to the backseat of the sport utility vehicle confirmed that his little slugger was still knocked out.

He'd fallen asleep almost as soon as David got him buckled into the child safety seat.

After a quick dash into his hotel room to retrieve the wallet he'd left on the dresser next to the television's remote control, he got a quart of orange juice and the medicine. David insisted on paying cash for the prescription—despite the pharmacist's assurance that it was free. The last thing he wanted to do was take away a resource from someone who actually needed it.

He roused Jeremy long enough to get him undressed, to the bathroom and back into the big bed. When they'd first checked in, the boy had loved the idea that he would get to sleep in a big bed like Daddy's. Jeremy had jumped on both double beds and giggled as he hopped from one to the other. But David knew he'd soon want to climb back into his own bed at home, the one decked out like a Formula One race car.

David stared down at his sleeping son as a concept that would enhance his presentation to city officials began unfolding in his mind.

Jeremy's bedroom furniture and the children's waiting room at the clinic had given him an idea. He picked up his sketchbook and settled on the sofa to make a few preliminary sketches. Liking where it was going, David fired up his computer and worked on a design for a green space that would meld nicely with a concept he had for a play on the old-style garden apartments that were popular in the 1970s and 1980s. He wrote *nouveau retro* in the margin on the sketchpad page, then created a computer file with the same name as the design ideas tumbled over each other.

Buzzing disturbed his train of thought.

David looked around, trying to determine the source of the noise. The television was on mute; a guy surrounded by fruits and vegetables and a perky blonde assistant hawked what, had the sound been up, he would have heard was the best juicer ever created on planet Earth.

Bzzz. Bzzz. Bzzz.

The radio on the nightstand between the beds glowed 11:20 p.m. He'd been working for a couple of hours and hadn't realized it.

Bzzz.

No sound came from the radio.

Jeremy had flung the light blanket off and was turned practically upside down on his bed, the sheets in a twist.

Then it dawned on him. The phone. He'd had it on vibrate and it was…where? He cast his gaze around the hotel room, wondering how he could lose something in a space the size of a studio apartment. Then he remembered. The counter in the bathroom. He'd put the phone down when they'd come in and gone straight to the toilet.

He padded his way over and decided to take the call there so Jeremy wouldn't be disturbed. He grabbed the phone before it fell to the floor after buzzing its way to the edge of the sink counter.

"Camden here."

"That's no way to answer the telephone. I've told you that at least a hundred times, dear."

David breathed a sigh that was both relief and exasperation. Charlotte Camden, his missing-in-action mother, had decided to check in. He'd left a couple of messages for her earlier in the day and hadn't heard a peep from her.

"Mom, where are you?"

"I'm at Becky's. She sends her love."

David rolled his eyes. The only thing his aunt Becky would send would be an order form for cookies or magazines or overpriced gift wraps and bows from one of the thousand civic group fund-raisers she always seemed to be in charge of. There were only so many peanuts and church cookbooks and happy cat calendars that a person could buy or tolerate.

"We had a lovely girls' day out," his mother said. "We went to a new spa here in Greensboro and had facials, and then we ate lunch at a cute little bistro…"

David leaned against the sink, rubbed his temple and sighed.

Here he was thinking she was having some sort of existential or menopausal crisis, and instead she was just hanging out with her sister.

"…and he asked me out to dinner. Imagine that!"

His eyes popped open, and he stood up. "What was that, Mom? Who? Dinner?"

A schoolgirl-sounding trill came through the mobile phone.

"He's in charge of the school district's transportation department. We're going to dinner and a movie. Isn't that nice?"

David shuddered and tried not to sigh again.

The thought of his mother dating gave him the heebie-jeebies. He knew it was unreasonable to expect that she would be alone the rest of her life. Charlotte Camden was not yet sixty years old and had already been a widow for almost a decade.

She didn't know that David thoroughly vetted the gentlemen friends she expressed interest in. And he'd confronted more than one who was after something other than the companionship of a lady of a certain age.

He knew he was overprotective when it came to his mother. Charlotte wasn't what might be called rich, but a trust left for her by his father in addition to a hefty insurance settlement after he'd died ensured that she would have no financial worries, and enough wealth to attract the sort looking for a gravy train.

"Yeah, lovely," he said of her dinner-date news.

What sounded like a moan from the other

room drew his attention. He pulled the bathroom door open a bit and listened.

"Daddy."

"I'm right here, buddy," he said, making his way to the beds.

"Is that Jeremy?" Charlotte asked. "What in the world is he doing up at this hour? David, you spoil him."

"He's sick, Mom. Can you hold on for a sec?"

He put the phone on his bed and sat on Jeremy's.

The boy crawled into his lap and moaned. His forehead was burning up.

David's heart started racing.

"Oh, boy."

"David! David!" The tinny voice floated from the phone.

He leaned over and snatched it up, cradling the phone in the crook of his neck. "Mom, I've got to go. I need to find a doctor."

"Find a doctor? What do you mean find a doctor? Call Dr. Johnson."

"Dr. Johnson is in Charlotte, mom. We're in Cedar Springs."

David eased Jeremy from his lap and back onto the bed, then dashed to the bathroom for a cool washcloth. He returned just a moment later with both the washcloth to press to his son's head and a glass of water.

"Cedar Springs? What in the...? Oh no! Oh, David, I'm so sorry. Was that this week? I thought you were going there next week."

Retching sounds were coming from Jeremy.

"Mom, I need to go."

He disengaged the phone and dashed for the wastebasket near the desk. He got back to Jeremy a second too late.

The boy started to cry. David didn't know if the tears were because his stomach hurt or because he'd just soiled his favorite Winnie the Pooh pajamas.

"It's gonna be okay, buddy."

David prayed that it would be as he comforted his son.

It was eleven thirty at night. He had two options. He could call 9-1-1 or he could call the doctor from the clinic. She'd written a number on the back of the business card she'd given Jeremy.

He put the wastebasket on the floor at the edge of the bed and cradled his son in one arm. With the other, he dug into his pocket and pulled out Dr. Spring Darling's business card.

Spring had just closed the book she'd been reading, turned off the bedside lamp, fluffed her pillows and settled in bed when her mobile phone chirped.

"Gerald, I am not giving you a prescription

for Valium," she muttered as she rolled over and reached for the telephone on the bedside table.

The burglars at Step Back in Time Antiques weren't after whatever they could grab. They'd come with a shopping list. Small but extremely valuable pieces were the only things missing from the antiques shop. If it hadn't been for a broken vase that Richard's wife had come across, they may not have even discovered the break-in for a day or two. She'd gotten the story from Gerald, the high-strung co-owner of the shop, while Richard, the more level-headed business partner, talked to police, then called their insurance company.

After checking on her friends, she'd driven to Cecelia's, where she'd stayed entirely too long for someone who had early morning rounds at the hospital. Gerald had already phoned twice asking for something to calm his nerves.

She didn't even glance at the caller ID on the phone. "Gerald, for the last time, I am not giving you a script for Valium. Drink some chamomile tea and go to bed."

"Uh, hello?"

Spring sat up and swung her legs over the side of the bed.

That rich baritone was *definitely* not Gerald Murphy on the line. It sounded like the man with the little boy who'd been at the clinic—the man she'd spent too much time talking about with Cecelia, the man whose voice did unreasonable things to her.

She turned on the light, then put on her professional voice. "I'm so sorry," she told her caller. "I thought it was a friend. This is Dr. Darling. To whom am I speaking?"

"I'm sorry for calling so late, doctor. It's David. David Camden. I brought my son in to see you earlier this evening."

Spring ran a hand through hair that tumbled in her face. She opened the bedside table drawer and pulled out a hair tie to tame it.

Putting the phone on speaker, she gathered up her hair and tugged it into a ponytail. "Is Jeremy all right?" she asked him.

"No."

She heard the panic in the man's voice and was up and headed to her closet for clothes to wear to either the clinic or the hospital.

"What are his symptoms?" she asked as she grabbed a pair of jeans and a white button-down shirt.

"He's burning up and throwing up. Hold on, please."

She stared at the phone for a moment. When she heard retching, her mind started running through what besides stomach flu might be wrong with the cute little boy. Spring pulled on the jeans and slipped into a pair of loafers.

"Dr. Darling? I'm back. He says his stomach hurts a lot. I didn't know who else to call."

"Where are you?"

When he told her, she was a bit surprised to hear that someone with financial troubles was living in that rather expensive hotel. There were several more economical options around town. But she said nothing about that. It wasn't her business. A sick child was her concern.

"I want you to take Jeremy to the hospital. To Cedar Springs General Hospital. I'll meet you there. Do you have something to write with? I can give you directions from where you are. It will take you less than ten minutes to get there."

She gave David the directions, shrugged on and buttoned her shirt and was about to grab her keys when she paused at the mirror. She made a quick detour to her large bathroom and applied a touch of powder and a bit of blush to her cheeks. She picked up a tube of lipstick, then frowned and put it back on the tray that held her makeup.

"It's a medical emergency, not a date," she said.

With her keys in hand, she grabbed her phone, the wallet clutch that held the essentials and the lanyard with her hospital IDs.

Outside, as she made her way to the garage,

she noticed the lights were still on at her mother's house. Spring's home was actually a separate wing of her mother's large estate. They shared the four-car garage on the property. Lovie Darling was a consummate entertainer, and the two cars in the drive, vehicles Spring didn't recognize, were proof of that.

In her Volvo car, Spring placed her hands on the steering wheel, closed her eyes and prayed for Jeremy Camden and his father.

Then she headed to the hospital. She hated that it was under these circumstances, but she found herself pleased at the prospect of seeing David Camden again.

Hot on the heels of that came the realization that her thoughts were inappropriate on so many levels. Chief among them was that there was most likely a Mrs. Camden who loved him and that precious little boy. But the doctor's suddenly sweaty hands and that little flutter in her gut gave evidence to another diagnosis—one of a far more personal nature.

For the first time in a long, long time, Spring found herself intrigued by a man, curious about his impression of her…and she fervently hoped there was no Mrs. Camden.

Chapter Four

Spring headed straight to the emergency department at Cedar Springs General Hospital. As one of the staff physicians at the medical center, she had a designated parking space and was able to bypass the entry used by other hospital employees.

On weekends, the emergency department—typically called an emergency room by the public, as if there was just one room to it—bustled with acute trauma cases, mostly of the do-it-yourself-home-improvement variety like broken arms and legs or fractures. Then there were the asthma attacks and bee stings, as well as the usual mix of possible heart attacks, allergic reactions to everything from peanuts to shellfish and the occasional car crash victim. Severe trauma patients who needed advanced care were airlifted to Durham, where specialists at Duke

University's emergency trauma hospital and facilities could handle burns, gunshot victims and the like. Thankfully, those cases were rare at Cedar Springs General.

Spring looked around but didn't see either David or Jeremy Camden in the emergency department's waiting room. This evening there was just a handful of people in the waiting area. Three people huddled together with a man who kept saying, "I'm not gonna let them touch me. I'm not gonna let them touch me." And an elderly woman in a light blue pantsuit sat erect in one of the chairs facing the receptionist's desk. The woman clutched her purse as if someone might try to snatch it from her grip.

The televisions were on; one wall-mounted plasma set displayed a cable news channel, while its twin depicted a late-night talk show host yukking it up with a celebrity guest.

"Hi, Dr. Darling," a man said from behind her. "What are you doing here this time of night?"

Spring turned to see Joseph Bradshaw, one of the physician assistants. Dressed in green scrubs, the uniform of most of the emergency department staff, he held a chart and was making his way toward one of the bays.

"Hi, Joseph. I got a call from the father of a patient. Acute abdominal pain that's gotten worse. They're supposed to meet me here."

"It's been pretty quiet tonight," Joseph said. "I haven't seen—"

Just then the automatic doors whooshed open and David Camden rushed in, almost running, with his son in his arms. The panic in his eyes and his bearing arrested Spring. He spotted her almost immediately.

"Dr. Darling!"

"Joseph, I'm going to need a bed."

"On it, Doc," he said, heading toward the emergency bays.

"He woke up doubled over," David said, approaching Spring. "And he threw up again."

"All right," Spring said as several emergency department aides rushed to take the boy.

"Daddy, my stomach hurts a lot," Jeremy said. Adding emphasis to just how much, the boy moaned and burrowed in closer to David's chest, instinctively seeking the protection of his father rather than the strangers with outstretched hands.

The sound tore at Spring. Little Jeremy's moan was one of the most pitiful sounds she had heard in a long, long time.

"Dr. Spring is right here," David told his son.

The boy lifted his head a bit. "Pretty Spring?"

"Yeah, buddy. It's Dr. Spring."

Despite the strain she saw evident in the worry lines at his mouth and brow, Spring heard a note of amusement in David's voice as he answered Jeremy. She'd been called many things in her thirty-five years, but this cute little boy calling her pretty just tugged at her heart.

It was clear Jeremy had more than just a bad case of stomach flu or too many jelly beans. Her mind raced with possibilities, none of them good.

"Noooo!" Jeremy cried out when David tried to place him on the gurney manned by two orderlies.

"It's okay, buddy," David assured his son, who resisted lying down. "I'm right here."

"Want Dr. Spring."

"I'm here, too, Jeremy," Spring said with a nod toward one of the orderlies. "If you'll lay back, we're going to take you into a room where I can see what's making your tummy hurt. Okay?"

The little boy nodded and did as she requested, but tears streaked down his face and he sought his father.

Spring glanced up at David.

"Can I come back?"

She nodded. "Of course."

Helpless and anxious, David watched as emergency room attendants wheeled his son into a room cordoned off with curtains and hooked him up to machines.

David was terrified, so he could only imagine

how Jeremy must feel. He reached deep for the anchor that would stabilize him. He needed to be strong for his son, not show the panic that raced through him. His heart beat so fast that he feared he might end up on a gurney next to Jeremy.

A moment later, he was politely asked by one of the attendants to step back.

"I can't leave my son."

A soft hand on his arm drew his attention. Spring was there.

"David, you don't have to. They just need some room to work."

He glanced around and saw a nurse or a doctor wheeling some sort of machine. He quickly moved to a spot she indicated, where he could stand and hold Jeremy's hand and not interfere with the tests they needed to run.

"Lord, you took her. Please don't take him, too," he whispered in an anguished plea. "He's all I have."

As she'd expected, the diagnosis wasn't good. Fortunately, it was something that was fairly routine for the hospital. Spring consulted with the emergency department's attending pediatrician while David Camden remained in the emergency room bay with Jeremy.

"We have done an ultrasound and a CT scan,"

Timothy Paquette, the department's pediatrician, told Spring.

Worried, Spring bit her lip. "I sent him home thinking it was just gastroenteritis."

"I would have done the same thing," Dr. Paquette said. "I took a look at the lab you did at the clinic. With his other symptoms, it made sense."

Spring nodded, but his words didn't make her feel any better. She just wanted to take Jeremy in her arms and hug all the hurt away.

"You want to talk to his father, or should I?" Paquette said. "Dr. Emmanuel should be here in about five minutes. The OR is ready just as soon as he gets here and the father gives the okay."

"I'll tell him," she said, knowing from experience the reaction he would have.

David jumped up from his chair when Spring entered the waiting room. Telling him his son was so sick wasn't going to be pleasant; this part of the job never was.

"Mr. Camden—"

"Call me David," he said, grabbing her hand. "Is Jeremy all right?"

He was clutching her hand so tightly that Spring winced.

He immediately dropped it. "I'm sorry. I'm just worried about Jeremy."

Spring resisted the urge to massage her throbbing hand. "He has appendicitis," she said. "Dr.

Adam Emmanuel is ready to operate once we get your approval."

"Operate? His appendix? But he's just four," David said.

"Appendicitis is not uncommon in children," Spring said. "Toddlers, even infants, can develop it. But it's harder to diagnose in the younger ones."

David Camden looked genuinely distressed. "Are you sure?"

Spring didn't know if his question was a result of her earlier misdiagnosis or the first and typical question from a worried parent of a sick child. Either way his question reminded Spring about their precarious financial situation. This was one of those situations where the generous donations to the Common Ground ministries paid off. The surgery Jeremy needed would not bankrupt his father or leave him with the choice between paying medical bills or paying to keep a roof over their heads, even if said roof was that of a hotel.

She nodded in answer to his question. "This is something that can't be ignored," she told him. "And it can't wait. If his infected appendix isn't removed, it could burst or leak, and that would lead to peritonitis, which can be fatal, particularly in children."

She didn't want to scare him, but he needed

to know all the facts to make an informed decision regarding his son's health.

David swallowed. His gaze connected with hers. She'd seen it before, the parents of her young patients looking in her eyes and trying to determine if she was leading them in the right direction.

"I…" David swallowed again, then took a deep breath and ran his hand over his face. "He's never been sick. Nothing like this. I just… Is he going to die?"

Spring's heart ached. She wanted to close her eyes and cry out at the arbitrariness of illness. But she maintained eye contact with him. "We need to get that appendix out as soon as possible."

"Was it something I did? The jelly beans?"

She placed her arm on his. "Mr. Camden… David, it's not your fault. It's not anyone's fault. There is no way to prevent appendicitis. It happens or it doesn't. All we can do is deal with it when it does occur. And Jeremy is in good hands. Dr. Emmanuel is board certified and our top pediatric surgeon."

He nodded.

"I know he's in good hands," David said. He looked away for a moment, as if embarrassed again, then met her gaze. Spring was sure he was going to ask how much the operation would cost.

"Dr. Darling, I don't know you, and I don't know if you're a woman of faith. But I need to pray right now. Will you join me?"

The question was not at all what she'd expected. But without a moment's hesitation, Spring nodded. That this man who had so much on him would ask a virtual stranger to pray with him said a lot about his character.

She bowed her head and a moment later felt his hand connect with hers. It was warm and strong and felt like an anchor in a storm. Given that he was the one in need, Spring could only marvel. When he began praying, she felt her own resolve grow stronger.

The surgery would last the better part of an hour. Parents, even the parent of a four-year-old, weren't allowed in the operating room. So rather than watch him pace the waiting room for an hour, Spring suggested they go to the hospital's cafeteria for a coffee.

Although open in the middle of the night with reduced kitchen staff, the cafeteria remained essentially empty with few people filling the gray-and-black aluminum chairs. Spring led the way across the room.

"Pardon the retro penitentiary waiting room look," she told David. "This part of the hospital, while open to the public, is used primarily by staff, so it's last on the renovation list. Patient rooms and family waiting rooms were the hospital administration's first priority."

Spring got a couple of coffees, and they settled at a table near the windows overlooking a courtyard in shadow.

"When the weather is nice," she said, "people like to go outside to eat or take a coffee break. The fresh air itself is medicinal, especially when you've been cooped up inside for hours."

She knew she was babbling, but she couldn't seem to help it. She was at a loss as to why she was so nervous. Over the course of her eight years at Cedar Springs General, she'd had hundreds of conversations with the parents of her patients, many of them in this very cafeteria. There was no reason for her heart to have such an erratic rhythm or for her hands to feel so clammy.

It was as if she were suddenly displaying symptoms of hypoglycemia or an anxiety attack. Since she was prone to neither, she had a pretty good idea of the cause of the rapid-onset malady.

"Mr. Camden—"

"David," he said.

Her mouth edged up in a slight smile, and she nodded. "David, Jeremy is in excellent hands with Dr. Emmanuel. He's one of the best in the region, and Jeremy's a trouper."

She watched as he looked about the room at

the empty tables. Across the cafeteria, a maintenance worker had parts of an ice machine's compressor on the floor and a couple of nurses were chatting as they sipped from tall tumblers.

"I guess I've been rather preoccupied lately." He stirred his coffee although he'd added neither cream nor sugar to it.

Spring wanted to, but she didn't ask the obvious question: preoccupied doing what? Whatever he wanted to tell her would come out in his own way.

"Jeremy has rarely been sick," he said. "He had a bit of colic when he was much younger, and he's had a couple of colds, but never anything that required being in the hospital, let alone an operation of any kind. I've been blessed that he's had good health."

When his gaze again connected with hers, Spring saw the beginning of panic in his eyes.

She reached out a hand and placed it on his arm in a gesture of comfort.

"I'm a grown man," he said, "and I've never had an operation. Not even my tonsils out. He has to be terrified. I should be—"

"You can't be in the operating room," she reminded him. "The procedure will take about an hour and a half. Dr. Emmanuel has barely gotten started. We'll be there in recovery when Jeremy wakes up. He needs you to be strong and focused. He's going to be sore for a while afterward."

David nodded. Then he wrapped his hands around the mug and contemplated the brown liquid in it. "I know." He exhaled as if releasing all the tension that had built up inside him. "I know," he said again.

Spring sipped at her coffee, letting the silence act as a balm to his tattered emotions.

"There's something you need to know," he said. "About me. Us, I mean. I'm not homeless. We're not homeless," he clarified.

"You don't have to—"

"Yes," he interrupted. "I do. I know you heard what happened at the clinic—about my insurance card. But I really did leave my wallet in the hotel room. I'm here in Cedar Springs for…for some business meetings. My sitter, who is my mother, is out of town. She had the dates of this trip mixed up. That's why Jeremy is with me. I don't normally have a four-year-old when I go on business trips."

"What type of business are you in?"

A buzzing sounded before he could answer her.

"Excuse me," Spring said, lifting a phone from her pocket. "I need to take this."

He nodded, and she answered. "This is Dr. Darling."

She listened for a moment, her eyes going wide. "Oh my. Okay, I'll be right up."

"What is it?" David asked. "Is Jeremy all right?"

She nodded to David and motioned for him to get up.

"Excellent," she told her caller. "I'll be there shortly."

"I'm sorry," she told him. "There's been an accident and they need another set of hands in the ER. I can show you the waiting room. It's quite comfortable."

While Jeremy was in surgery and Dr. Darling doctored or did whatever she did, David had plenty of time to pace and pray, stress and worry. The time seemed to pass with the pace of a glacier. Every time he glanced at his watch or the clock on the wall, barely five minutes had ticked by. He eventually sat down and closed his eyes, leaning his head back as he contemplated first the ceiling and then the wall.

"David, I am so sorry!"

His eyes popped open, and he blinked, not at all sure he was seeing her.

Charlotte Camden rushed into the waiting room in a flurry of silk and chiffon, her signature scarves trailing behind her in a flutter of femininity.

He rose as she approached. And a moment later, David found himself enveloped in the scent of Shalimar, the perfume she'd worn with a light touch his entire life. As a young child, he'd known that scent meant comfort and love. It was forever connected with his senses as maternal love, the way a mother should smell.

For just a moment, David was transported to the time when he was nine and his cocker spaniel, Chuckle Boy, had been hit by a car. He'd been inconsolable. The dog had been his best friend since Chuckle Boy was a puppy. His mother wrapped her arms around him, murmuring words of comfort, words meant to make him feel better. But there was nothing that could console him, not when he had to say goodbye to the dog that had meant the world to him.

Now he wondered if his son had any similar sensory triggers. Would Jeremy grow up never knowing a mother's embrace? Would he end up dreading the scent of a hospital?

He'd just met her this evening, but David knew he was quickly coming to crave the scent of Spring Darling. It wasn't so much a perfume, more her essence.

David held on to his mother, drawing from her what strength he could. But he was no longer a little boy. His mother couldn't kiss the boo-boos and make them better. He was a grown man with a little boy of his own. And even though his gut was tied in knots worrying about Jeremy, David knew everything possible was being done to get his son well and whole again.

Drawing his mother's hand into his, he led her to one of the sofas.

"It's okay, Mom."

"It's not okay," Charlotte moaned. "I'm mortified. I left Becky's right after we got off the phone and drove straight to the hotel. The front desk clerk told me you'd rushed Jeremy to the hospital. I was frantic with worry. I can't believe I let you down like this. And my baby! How is my baby?" Her voice rose along with her panic.

He knew how she must be feeling. If it was anything at all like the way he was feeling at the moment, it was borderline hysteria coupled with a megadose of surrealism. He'd been lucky. Jeremy, unlike other kids, had not suffered the early childhood ailments like ear infections or croup or whopping cough.

"The doctors say it's his appendix."

"But he's only four," Charlotte protested. "He's just a baby."

"I know," David said. "I thought the same thing. But the doctor said it's not uncommon."

Just then Spring entered the waiting room. Although three other people were there now, waiting for word on their own loved ones, her gaze found his almost immediately.

David met her halfway. "Is there any news?"

"He's heading up to recovery," she said. "He'll be out of it, groggy from the anesthesia, but he's going to be fine, David. He's going to be just fine."

David swooped her up into his arms and twirled her around. He planted a kiss on her mouth. "Thank you. Thank you."

Spring's joy mirrored his own, and even as he set her on her feet, he led her toward Charlotte.

"Mom, this is one of Jeremy's doctors. Dr. Spring Darling is the pediatrician I took him to."

"Well," Charlotte said with an assessing glance at Spring, "I can't say I ever greeted *your* pediatrician like that."

David gave her a blank look and then whipped his head around to Spring, his eyes widening as the realization of what he'd done sank in.

"I'm sorry," he said, releasing her hand as if it were suddenly molten lava. "I got caught up in the moment."

Spring sent a professional smile his way, as if all the parents of her patients kissed her like that. "No problem," she said. She extended her hand to the older woman. "It's a pleasure to meet you, Mrs.—"

"Camden," Charlotte supplied, shaking the doctor's hand. "Believe it or not, it's the same as my son's."

Spring tucked her hands in the pockets of her lab coat. "In my line of work, I never assume anything."

Charlotte's shrewd gaze seemed to assess Spring, and David realized with a jolt that he needed to cut off her speculation before it went too far. Dr. Spring Darling had shown not a whit of interest in him. Her concern, and rightly so, had been solely on Jeremy.

"I suppose that's right," Charlotte said. "Thank you for the news about my grandson. Do you have children?"

"Uh, Mom, I'm sure Dr. Darling has some other rounds to make. Can we see him?"

"I'll show you the way," she said.

Jeremy lay in a hospital bed in the pediatric recovery ward, looking much smaller and younger than he already was.

Going to his son, David brushed the hair back from the boy's forehead. "Hey there, champ. You came through. To God be the glory."

Jeremy turned toward his father's voice, but otherwise he didn't stir.

"He'll come around in about ten minutes," Spring assured him.

And when he did, David knew his son would be delighted to see his pretty Dr. Spring waiting to greet him.

"May I talk with you a moment?" Charlotte Camden asked Spring.

If she was surprised by the request, Spring didn't show it. "Of course," she said, leading her to the waiting room down the hall. The two sat, Spring facing the older woman. David Camden had his mother's eyes, and she could see some of his other features in her face.

"Thank you for caring for my son and grandson," Charlotte said. "This is all my fault. I was supposed to be watching Jeremy. This never would have happened if I'd paid more attention."

"Mrs. Camden, appendicitis isn't anyone's fault. It just happens," Spring assured her just as she had David. "It could have happened anywhere at any time. There's nothing you or Mr. Camden could have done."

Charlotte didn't look convinced. If anything, Spring thought, she looked more worried than she had just a few seconds ago.

"He's under an incredible amount of stress," Charlotte said as she fingered the edge of one dangling scarf. "I just wish I could do more for him."

Since Spring didn't know what the Camden

situation was, she could only make the kinds of sounds that could be perceived as comforting.

With little else that she could tell the distressed grandmother, she made a suggestion that Charlotte get a cup of coffee or tea.

"Thank you, but no. I'll wait here," Charlotte said. "I'd like to see Jeremy again when I can. I should have been here. I was getting a massage while my grandson was in terrible pain."

Spring knew nothing about this family, their situation or relationships, so she couldn't offer the woman any assurances one way or the other. She was awfully curious.

But the nature of a hospital physician's interaction with patients meant the back stories and the how it all worked out or even came to be were rarely, if ever, known after discharge. The same would be true of the Camdens once Jeremy was up and around and feeling better.

"Sure," Spring said. "That won't be a problem."

A few minutes later, she saw Jeremy Camden and again wondered if there was another Mrs. Camden in his life.

Spring found she had not been able to stop thinking about the father and son duo, even after all the unexpected extra hours in the emergency department, getting home and going straight to bed.

Three mornings a week she worked out at F.I.T. gym with her sister. Today, though, she'd begged off after promising that she'd run five miles to make up for it. She'd had specific and necessary errands to run before going to the hospital. There had been a place at Commerce Plaza she needed to visit.

As she walked into the hospital, she carried a two-foot-tall brown teddy bear sporting a natty red-and-white-polka-dot bow tie around his neck.

She wasn't in the habit of buying gifts for her patients. Like many service professionals who worked with children, she kept a stock of small toys like yo-yos and coloring books with crayons to give to kids, but nothing like this plush bear that was built well and meant to last a lifetime.

Spring was so thankful that Jeremy had come through the surgery and recovery with flying colors. She knew that she was getting emotionally involved. But she couldn't help it.

Jeremy Camden was now recuperating in a patient room in the pediatric wing of the hospital.

She tapped on the partially open door, heard "come in" and entered the little boy's room.

"Dr. Spring!" the boy exclaimed when he saw

her. He struggled to sit up, then let out an "Ow" and leaned back.

"Easy, Jeremy," Charlotte Camden admonished her grandson while rising from the chair near the boy's bed. "You're supposed to be resting."

Charlotte pushed the mechanism that raised the bed so Jeremy could sit up.

"Is that for me?" the boy asked, eyeing the teddy bear.

"It sure is," Spring said. "But you have to do what Dr. Emmanuel and your grandmother say."

"I am. Gonna have a sore," he said, tugging at the small hospital gown so she could see as she approached.

"A scar, Jeremy," his grandmother corrected.

Spring ruffled the boy's hair and handed him the bear, which Jeremy immediately hugged.

"He's almost as big as me!"

The delight on his face assured her that she'd done the right thing in buying and giving it to him. "He sure is," Spring said.

"What do you say?" Charlotte prompted him.

With one small arm flung around the stuffed animal, Jeremy reached for Spring with the other. The hug came naturally to him. It was awkward with the bed rail, the IV and the bear, but so worth it when he said in her ear, "Thank you—I love him."

"How are you feeling?" she asked as she checked his readings on the monitors near the bed and on his chart. Everything looked good and so did he.

"I get to stay here in the hospital!"

Spring smiled.

"Only a child would see that as a good thing," Charlotte said with a laugh.

Only a child who was never or rarely sick, Spring amended silently. Now came the recuperation period, and she knew from experience that if he was feeling better, he'd be itching to run around like a little boy with boundless energy.

"Because it was so late when David brought him in, the doctor said they'd like to keep Jeremy for a full day of observation."

Spring wondered where David Camden was. The nurses said he hadn't left his son's side since he'd come out of surgery.

"You just missed David," Charlotte said as if reading Spring's mind. "I sent him to the hotel to get some proper rest. He has a business meeting later today and several tomorrow morning and needs to be ready for them. We'll probably both end up staying the night."

"Oh." Spring was surprised at the deflated feeling that rushed through her, but she responded to the older woman. "Yes. That's good."

Then she questioned her own actions and

second-guessed her motives. Had she brought Jeremy a gift simply to be able to see his father again?

No, she realized. When she saw the bear, her first thought had simply been the towheaded little boy who'd been in so much pain and had been such a trouper.

"Dr. E said I can go home after today and Grandma's gonna stay at the hotel. Then we go home later," Jeremy reported.

Spring was still confused about the whole business concerning the hotel versus the house, but she wasn't about to question Mrs. Camden. She'd already gathered from what David had said and from the quality of Mrs. Camden's clothing that they were not in the financial trouble she'd imagined.

"I checked with Jeremy's pediatrician in Charlotte. He suggested a day of bed rest after he's released rather than a road trip home."

"And Charlotte is home?"

Charlotte Camden nodded and then smiled. "I was named for the city and for an aunt. I know it gets confusing sometimes. David's company is based there. I'm the grandma in chief on the board of directors."

David's company.

The words should have been a comfort, should have taken away the uncertainty and assured her that he had spoken the truth. Instead they made Spring feel as if she were suddenly treading water near a rip current.

She had been attracted to him from the moment she'd set eyes on him. And Spring Darling had no room in her heart for attraction and what it tended to do to the emotions. She had been down that path before, and it led straight to disaster. No, she reasoned, being attracted to a person was merely a chemical response in the body, dopamine and testosterone responding to like receptors in the other person—something any first-year medical student knew. It didn't have to mean anything else. But none of that reasoning explained the arc of fear that lanced through her now.

What if they began a relationship? And what if he lied to her the way Keith had? She had given her heart once before only to have it thoroughly and utterly trounced. Crushed by a man she'd trusted and thought she'd loved, a man she had been ready to marry.

That made her think of her sister's upcoming engagement party, an event Spring knew she would have to attend no matter how much it hurt. She was truly happy for Summer and knew that in Cameron Jackson her sister had found a man of strong faith and character. Summer and

Cameron weren't responsible for the heartsick memories their happiness invoked in her.

"Dr. Darling, are you all right?"

Spring blinked. Mrs. Camden's gentle hand rested on her arm as if holding her steady.

She forced a smile and nodded. "I'm fine. Really," she added as if to assure herself rather than the other woman.

"For a second there you looked in pain."

"My thoughts just drifted for a moment."

Straight down a rabbit hole, she thought. Spring wasn't given to flights of fancy or romantic notions. She was the straight-arrow Darling sister, the one totally focused on career and community. So she didn't know where the scenario of a relationship had sprung from.

David Camden was the parent of a patient... and he'd planted a kiss on her that she still remembered, felt and wished to experience again.

"Dr. Spring?"

Her focus shifted again to her young patient. "Yes?"

"What should I name my bear?"

Spring cocked her head a bit, considering the little boy and the bear almost as big as he was. "Well," she said. "He's wearing a bow tie. So how about Beau? B-E-A-U," she added for his benefit.

Jeremy's face lit up. "Okay. I like that. Hi,

Beau," he said, giving the bear a kiss. He then hugged it to him and closed his eyes. A moment later, he was sound asleep.

Charlotte smiled down at her grandson. "He and his father are the joys of my life," she said.

"You're blessed to have both of them," Spring said, realizing that she truly meant the words. They were not merely the sort of pleasant platitude or banal cliché offered when two strangers conversed or when a doctor was trying to be pleasant with a patient's family.

Knowing it wasn't protocol, but unable to stop herself, Spring bent and placed a kiss on Jeremy's head, then said goodbye to Charlotte.

With Jeremy on her mind and a quiet prayer of thanksgiving on her heart, she slipped from his hospital room, turned right and collided with David Camden.

Chapter Five

"I'm sorry," Spring said as her sparkling blue eyes widened and a blush crept up her cheeks.

"My fault," David said at the same time.

He had been thinking about Dr. Spring Darling only to have the pretty physician walk straight into his arms. He steadied her, then let go quickly even though he wanted to breathe in the scent of her hair and hold her for just a moment. Since neither was appropriate, he held up a now partially crumpled piece of paper.

"I was headed to the hotel when I glanced at this and realized I needed some clarification from the nurses."

"Let me see," Spring offered. "I may be able to help."

Although they were no longer in physical contact, neither of them moved from the spot where they'd collided.

Her eyes, he decided, were the blue of a cloud-less summer day, and her lashes were full and long.

"Your eyelashes are beautiful."

As soon as the inane words left his mouth, David felt as if he were fifteen and trying to ask Cindy Rae, his longtime secret crush, if he could walk her home from vacation Bible school. What type of lame guy complimented a woman on her eyelashes?

But instead of the "Well, bless your naive lit-tle heart for even thinking you had a shot with me" look that Cindy Rae had given him all those years ago, Spring Darling actually smiled. He watched as her eyes lit up with genuine humor and not the amused pity of a pageant princess in the making. The smile that now curved Spring's mouth was the very one that he'd dreamed about while dozing on the chair in Jeremy's room.

"I'm the envy of my younger sisters, who spend hundreds of dollars every year on eye-lash plumpers, lash curlers and every new mas-cara that hits the market."

"Brains and beauty," he said almost to himself. "Now there's a lethal combination."

"I'm as tame as they come," she said. "Would you like me to take a look at the instructions?"

After taking half a step back from her to clear his head, as well as put some physical distance between them, David smoothed the paper on his pants leg before handing it to her.

"Dr. Emmanuel is going to release him tomorrow," he told her. "I asked for instructions early so I could get anything he might need and have it ready."

"Jeremy's just fallen asleep," Spring said. "We can talk in the atrium. It's right down the hall."

He glanced at Jeremy's closed hospital door. Even though he'd left barely half an hour ago, he couldn't resist checking to make sure he was resting comfortably. "I'll just take a quick look."

Spring nodded, and he thought she might be used to anxious parents who wanted to assure themselves that their little ones fared well. "I'll wait here."

Charlotte glanced up from the newspaper she was reading in the very chair where David had spent the night. She smiled and lifted a finger to her mouth. "Shh."

He nodded.

Jeremy was indeed sleeping, looking as he always did. Were it not for the hospital bed, the monitors and a huge teddy bear that he was clutching, his son would have looked as if he were at home in his own bed. The life-size bear sported a polka-dot bow tie and was just the sort of toy David would have gotten for him had his mind been on anything but the surgery his little boy had undergone.

"That was a good idea," he told his mom with a nod toward Jeremy's new companion. "Thank you."

Charlotte shook her head. "Not from me. It's from Dr. Darling."

David's brow lifted in surprise. "Really?"

She nodded, then whispered, "He named it Beau for the bow tie."

David didn't know what to make of this news, but he was grateful to see Jeremy looking so peaceful following the trauma of the previous night. After coming out of recovery and waking, he'd been fretful and the night had been long. The nurses told him that it was normal for children to be anxious in the unfamiliar surroundings.

"I'm going to talk to the doctor," he said, still keeping his voice low so Jeremy wouldn't be disturbed.

"All right, dear," his mother said. "I'll be right here."

David leaned over the bed rail and kissed the top of his son's head. Then, after sending a smile his mother's way, he returned to the hall, missing Charlotte's speculative glance at him.

Spring Darling was still there, not that he'd expected her to disappear. Her head was lowered in the position that he'd starting calling "Americans and their best friends" as she tapped on her phone. She must have sensed him standing there because she looked up. And when she smiled, David's breath caught.

Her beauty was refined and classic, putting him in mind of pearls and calla lilies, rather than, say, daisies and bare feet, though no flowers or jewelry save a watch and small gold posts adorned her. No gold band was on her left hand, and he had the impression she would be the type of woman who would display her union with that symbol. He realized that he was interested in getting to know her…and that interest had nothing at all to do with the fact that she'd come to his son's aid last night even though the clinic was officially closed.

"We can talk in the atrium," she said again.

With that comment, David realized that Dr. Spring Darling was a pediatrician and her business was medicine. She was just doing her job, seeing to patients and ready to answer any questions parents had about care.

Then what was the teddy bear all about, he wondered to himself.

Spring wasn't quite sure how it happened. One minute they were headed to the atrium, and the next she was suggesting the patio terrace of a coffeehouse near the hospital instead. She told herself that the atrium was crowded with patients and their families getting a bit of morning sun, but knew that wasn't the full reason behind her decision.

Like a moth to a flame, something about David Camden called to her, beckoned her. And instead of activating the emotional shields she erected whenever a man got too close or seemed interested in her, she opened herself to the possibilities. If she wasn't mistaken, she'd seen a spark in his eyes that mirrored her own when it came to him.

It was an intriguing and unique situation for her. And she was a grown woman. As her youngest sister, Autumn, would say, "Life's too short to miss the game. Play ball!"

So she and David Camden settled on the patio terrace of the coffee shop that was a gravel pathway away from Cedar Springs General Hospital. The spot, frequented by hospital staff and employees from the nearby medical office complex, buzzed with the midmorning chatter of people taking quick breaks or grabbing an early lunch before dashing back to cubicles, labs and patients.

"Thank you," David said. "For the teddy bear you gave Jeremy."

Spring felt her cheeks grow warm and knew

she couldn't attribute it to the skinny chai latte she sipped. "I saw it and thought of him. He seemed to like it."

Silence fell between them then, as though they both searched for words to fill the space. Instead of being awkward, the shared contemplation seemed comfortable to Spring. It even, she dared think, felt right. As if they'd done this many times before. And before she knew it, she'd voiced just that idea.

He smiled. "I thought it was just me."

Well, Spring surmised. *Well, well, well.*

After taking another sip of her latte, she nodded toward the papers from Adam Emmanuel that David had placed on the table. "Dr. Emmanuel's instructions are spot-on," she told him. "After discharge tomorrow, Jeremy will need bed rest. You'll know he's ready to resume his normal schedule when he's fidgeting to get out of bed or says he's hungry."

He smiled. "That would be always," he said. "And spoken from experience I take it. How many children do you have?"

"About three hundred," she said. "But I loan them out to their other parents for extended periods of time."

That earned a laugh from him, and Spring liked the way it sounded, as if a well of good humor lived deep within him and he tapped it often.

"I know it was scary," she said.

"Terrifying."

"But he came through like an ace."

David nodded. "With a lot of praying and deal making with God."

Curious about that, she asked the obvious follow-up question. "What did you offer?"

"Everything," David said. "My job keeps me busy, and being a single father has its challenges. I didn't know—or maybe it's that I didn't realize how easy it was to prioritize until now. Jeremy comes first."

"Your mother said she's going to stay with him."

He nodded. "She got the adjoining room at the hotel and will stay for a day or two, then take Jeremy home while I finish up here."

"What's your work?" she asked.

"Ah, so you finally believe I'm a productive member of society? I'm an architect," he said. "If you'd like, I can have someone from my office scan and email my degrees and licenses to prove it."

Her cheeks grew warm again, a recurring affair around this man, but this time she knew the cause was embarrassment. "I'm sorry."

He shrugged, then flashed a grin that was

quick and easy. "When I had an objective moment to think about it in the middle of the night, I had to laugh. We must have been quite a sight at the Common Ground clinic. The clerk at the front desk directed me there as the closest and best place to get medical treatment."

"I'm glad, then," she said, even though she knew her words could and probably would be interpreted as flirting. Spring couldn't remember the last time she'd flirted with a man.

"Me, too," he said. "We got the best doctor in town."

With a start, she realized that he was flirting with her.

As they enjoyed their beverages, David told her a funny story about Jeremy and a stuffed dinosaur he'd gotten after a visit to the natural history museum.

"The next thing I know, I'm trying to convince him that monsters are not under the bed or in the closet trying to eat him. In retrospect, a dinosaur exhibit may have been a bit much for a three-year-old. The ones at the museum were not purple and cuddly."

She was barely able to keep the laughter from her voice as she told him, "I know for a fact it was too much for a little girl who was six years old."

"You?"

Spring shook her head. "My sister Summer. I was fifteen and she was six when we had to douse the entire house with monster spray before she would settle down."

"Amazing things, those spray bottles filled with water," he said with a grin.

"I wish it had just been water," Spring said. "I added a couple of drops of green food coloring and made up a label that said, 'Certified by the Dinosaur Society of America' to lend it authenticity. Summer stopped crying and went to sleep assured that our house was safe from dinosaurs that liked to munch on little girls. Unfortunately, Mother didn't appreciate the pale green tint added to her silk-covered throw pillows and dry-clean-only draperies."

"How much trouble did you get into?"

"I had to pay for the cleaning out of my allowance and I was banned from doing any more educational babysitting."

"Wait a minute," he said. "Did you say your sister's name is Summer?"

Spring groaned. "I wondered if you'd caught that. We were the objects of much amusement for a while." She lifted a hand before he could say anything else. "There's also a Winter and an Autumn."

She saw his eyes widen, and Spring knew he was trying to wrap his head around the fact that the four sisters were named for the seasons. His grin grew broader.

"Collectively, we were called The Seasons of Love or, more familiarly, simply The Seasons."

"Okay," he said around a sip of his coffee. "I'll bite. Why?"

"Why were we called The Seasons, or why were we named by obvious lunatics?" The amusement in her voice conveyed that she bore no real ill will toward said lunatics.

He seemed to be trying to hold the chuckles in, and he just waved a hand in a go-on-with-the-story expansive motion.

"My mother's name is Louvenia, but every-one calls her Lovie. Hence, The Seasons of Love. And that little sister who was certain that a di-nosaur would come to life and that she would be its midnight snack is all grown-up and getting married soon."

David cocked his head and studied her for a moment. "Why does that bother you?"

Spring's breath caught. "I beg your pardon?"

"Your sister Summer," he said. "Her upcom-ing wedding bothers you."

"Wh-what would make you say such a thing?"

He shrugged and sat back. "The light. In your eyes, I mean. It seemed to dim a bit when you said she's getting married soon. Is the groom-to-be not quite up to what you'd hoped for your little sister?"

Spring cleared her throat and reached for her latte cup, only to discover it empty. She glanced around, looking for an out, for a way not to get into this. Finding none, she opted for the only option open to her.

"I…I have to leave now," she said. "I'm sorry to have kept you so long. Your mother said you had to prepare for business meetings."

Spring rose, knowing that she was being cool and rude but unable to stop herself.

This man she'd known all of a day had taken one look at her and discerned the secret she thought she hid so well.

Her younger sister had been widowed two years ago, had moved home to Cedar Springs from Georgia and promptly found and fallen in love with Cameron Jackson, the town's fire chief.

It wasn't fair.

Life wasn't fair, and Spring knew at the heart of it she *was* happy for her sister. Summer had been through a lot and more than deserved any and every happiness she could find. Summer had overcome emotional barriers that Spring didn't think she, the eldest of the Darling girls, would have been able to handle if put in the same set of circumstances.

"I didn't mean to upset you," David said.

She glanced at the hand on her arm, then realized that David was standing, as well—and looking alarmed in a way that made her feel even more inadequate.

Boy, would her friends be stunned to discover that under the take-charge, always-in-control facade, Dr. Fixit and all-around community activist, Spring Darling, MD, was really a woman afraid that she had missed her opportunities at happiness, at finding love and a family of her own. She was, after all, thirty-five years old, and Cedar Springs, North Carolina, was not the East Coast's hotbed of romantic possibilities for older single women.

Maybe it was being around young mothers and their children all day that made her feel old, that made Spring wonder why it seemed so easy for others to find their forever mates. All she'd ever attracted were men like Keith Henson who were more interested in her trust fund and wealth than in what she offered as an individual.

She cast stricken eyes up at David. "I... You didn't," she finally managed to stammer even as she felt tears gathering. Tears that she could not—would not—shed here. "I do need to go, though." She glanced at her watch as if to emphasize the point. "Thank you for the latte."

Spring walked quickly toward the door, glad that they'd walked to the coffee shop and that she wouldn't need to be in the confined space of a car with him for even a few minutes.

It was close to one in the afternoon now and even though she was fleeing the scene like a criminal caught in the act but still certain of escape, she realized that she and David Camden had sat talking for close to an hour.

Without turning back to see if he was watching her hasty departure, Spring almost ran across the pathway and to the hospital lot where she'd parked her dependable Volvo car.

She fumbled with the key fob and eventually scrambled in and sat behind the wheel, trying to steady her emotions and her rapidly beating heart.

Too close.

He'd gotten too close to the truth she didn't want to acknowledge to herself, let alone reveal to someone else.

Almost hyperventilating, the doctor thought she might be having a panic attack. Instead of consulting a fellow medical practitioner, she did what any normal person would do: she called her best friend.

Despite having assured his mother that he would get some rest, prepare for his meetings and not worry about Jeremy, David was at the hospital for his son's release the next morning.

Knowing that Jeremy was going to be all right afforded him the opportunity to focus on his first meeting, which was just a prelude to the one where he knew the opposition would be lying in wait.

After seeing Jeremy and his mother comfortably ensconced at the hotel, he checked his notes one final time.

"Don't worry about us, dear," his mother said. "You go make a good impression on those people."

He suspected that the eyedrops he'd used to mask the lack of sleep did little for the bags he sported under his eyes. There was little he could do about that now, though, as he approached the Cedar Springs city hall building for his first meeting of the day, this one with the city's police and fire chiefs, Zachary Llewelyn and Cameron Jackson, respectively. He was glad they had requested late morning instead of first thing. The chiefs had other appointments at eight and at nine, so eleven o'clock was deemed ideal and ended up being perfect for David.

David checked in at the reception desk and accepted a visitor badge that he clipped to his suit jacket's lapel. The media reports he'd read suggested this meeting with the public-safety chiefs would be easy compared with the midafternoon planning commission meeting. Although held in the middle of the afternoon on a workday, *that* meeting would be packed, according to an article in the *Cedar Springs Gazette.*

David presented himself at the office where he'd been directed and introduced himself to the clerk there.

"Oh, hello, Mr. Camden. I'm Gloria Reynolds—I spoke with you earlier. It's nice to put a face to the voice and emails," she said. "Chief Llewelyn is here and Chief Jackson just arrived. Right this way."

She showed him into a small conference room that had a table, four chairs and a slim credenza holding a carafe. "The coffee is hot, and the crullers are fresh from Sweetings," she told him. Then, raising her voice so it carried across the room to the credenza where the refreshments were set up, she added, "You'd better hurry, though, before a certain police chief, who shall remain unnamed, gobbles them all up."

"I do resemble that description, Gloria," rumbled a big man, who'd turned at her voice. "Jackson's getting married soon, so he has to watch his svelte figure. That leaves more for me."

Shaking her head, the clerk walked to the door. "Just let me know if you need anything," she said before pulling it closed.

David immediately felt at ease with these two men. The police chief had a good twenty years and thirty pounds on him, but he had the look of ex-military and kept himself in shape. This was no stereotypical big-bellied Southern cop. It was the fire chief, however, who was the surprise. David pegged the man for about his age or a bit younger, which would put him in his early thirties and therefore fairly young to be a chief of anything.

"Thanks for meeting with me," David said as introductions were made and handshakes went around. When all three were at the table with coffees prepared, the police chief started dunking a cruller in his.

"If you've been reading that weekly rag they call a newspaper here, it's a wonder you even showed up, Camden," Llewelyn said.

And with that comment, David knew that he had at least one ally, if not a friend in the city's administrative ranks.

"Zach," Cameron Jackson said, "we're not here to talk politics."

The warning in the fire chief's voice told David that if he thought he had an ally in the police chief, the same couldn't necessarily be said for fire chief Jackson. But the big man just rolled his eyes.

"If you haven't figured it out yet," Llewelyn said, "Chief Cam here is the good chief, and I'm the bad one."

"Ignore him," Cameron Jackson said. "He's still smarting because my firefighters beat his cops at softball last weekend."

"He had a ringer on his team," the police chief said, as if David were a judge and jury and the two chiefs lawyers arguing their cases.

"Autumn Darling is on the firefighters' auxiliary."

"Humph," the police chief grunted. "An *auxiliary* formed a week before the game." He pointed his cruller at David to make his point. "His soon-to-be sister-in-law is a coach. She excels at baseball, basketball, tennis, field hockey and rugby, to name just a few. And if that's not bad enough, she owns a torture center she calls a gym. That sound like a ringer to you?"

While the police and fire chief chuckled and bantered good-naturedly, David sat reeling over something the police chief had said.

Darling. Again. Another one?

Even if Darling were a common last name in Cedar Springs, there could be no doubt that Autumn Darling was Dr. Spring Darling's sister—one of The Seasons of Love. The probability of Cedar Springs or any other city having two residents with that particular first and last name were about negative three hundred to one.

What he needed to know, and right this minute, was which Darling was the one opposed to the project he was hoping to bring to fruition in the city.

"Darling?" he said. "I've seen that name in some of the media reports."

Chief Zachary Llewelyn chuckled. "That would be Lovie Darling, also known as Cedar Springs' force to be reckoned with. But she thinks the sun rises and sets on Chief Cam there," he said.

David was pretty sure he already knew what these men were about to confirm, but he asked the question that was expected of him. "Why is that?"

The police chief grinned as he finished off the cruller, then cupped his hands around his coffee mug, which had CSPD emblazoned on it. "He's marrying one of Lovie's girls."

"Zach, I really don't think Mr. Camden came all the way over here from Charlotte to talk about my marital status. You have some numbers you wanted to share with us, right, Mr. Camden?"

The police chief gave David a conspiratorial wink, then lifted from the empty seat a large municipal binder that indicated he was ready to focus on business now.

"Please, call me David," he said, even as he tried to reconcile how all the familial connections might play out with regard to a mixed-use development in the city.

He'd done his research and knew that Cedar Springs was more small city than small town. While it was nowhere near the size of metropolitan Charlotte, he hadn't anticipated working in an environment where everyone—least of all the people he would be working with—were related. Lovie Darling was the vocal opposition in the local newspaper. The city's fire chief was about to marry into the Darling family. And to put yet another plump and juicy cherry on top of his quickly melting professional sundae, Dr. Spring Darling, a woman who under other circumstances he would be mighty interested in getting to know, had saved Jeremy's life.

He was fighting an uphill battle, and he knew it. If there hadn't been a lot of people depending on him, he would have just counted the entire effort a loss. Maybe Jeremy's illness had been a sign from on high that this project was not meant to be.

But that test had been met, and he knew that he and his team, the people back at Carolina Land Associates, were depending on him to close the deal and keep the company operating. He couldn't let his attraction to Spring Darling and her family's opposition to his work deter him.

"From what we understand from Mayor Howell," Cameron Jackson said, "you want to get an idea of what additional emergency services would be needed given a number of different development scenarios."

Forcing himself to get his mind off the pretty doctor with the complicated family ties and on the meeting, David nodded as he pulled from his own briefcase a large three-ring binder and an electronic tablet.

"I'm here to site three locations. I received from the city manager's office—"

"More likely from the mayor's office," the police chief interjected. "She's the one pushing this thing."

David tapped on the tablet and three dialog boxes popped up, images from the deck of slides he planned to present during the planning commission meeting. "Well, I got from the city a list of six locations. My staff has done some groundwork, and we've narrowed it to three. I'm here to follow up on the primary one they recommended, which," he added, "also happens to coincide with the mayor's preferred site."

"Lovie Darling's land," Zachary Llewelyn said.

"Actually," Cameron inserted, "the land in question belongs in trust to the sisters, equal shares and acres for each."

"Is acquiring the land going to pose a problem?" David asked.

The two chiefs glanced at each other. Cameron Jackson sighed.

"Put it like this, David," Llewelyn said. "Given what happened at last month's city council meeting, I think I'll loan you a Kevlar vest to wear to the planning commission meeting this afternoon."

Spring had arranged her schedule so she could attend the city's planning commission meeting. Members of the Cedar Springs Historical Society had learned the hard way about the work and scope of the planning commission. It was here, not at city council, where things began to happen. Zoning changes were approved here. Permits were reviewed and either accepted or rejected. New businesses and enterprises that wanted to open, expand or relocate in the city started the process here. More times than not, by the time a project came before the city council, it was all but a done deal. Only the aesthetics remained to be hashed out before the council, and it was too late for substantive changes or for anyone with an opposing voice to be heard.

So the historical society, represented by Spring, her mother, Lovie Darling, and other members were there to monitor the proceedings.

Spring had the number of the historical society's volunteer attorney on speed dial. Given the way Mayor Howell had slipped a previous development project by the voters and the historical society, they were ready with a motion for an injunction on anything the mayor may have convinced a majority of the planning commissioners to do.

She hoped it wouldn't come to that. She was a person of peace, a woman who'd sworn an oath to do no harm.

"Let's sit in the middle," Lovie suggested. "I want to be able to hear and see everything."

"Lead the way," Spring said, allowing her mother to pass.

Three of the five planning commission members were already seated at the two long tables in the front of the multipurpose room. Unlike the Cedar Springs City Council, the planning commission didn't have chambers for its meetings, and, by mayoral decree, commission and committee gatherings weren't permitted in city council chambers even though the space went unused during the day. The commission, these men and women who worked behind the scenes and had their actions mostly rubber-stamped by the council, were instead relegated to a multipurpose room at city hall.

Several rows of blue-cushioned chairs were arranged in lecture hall fashion for the public and interested parties. During the holiday season, the room was festooned with greenery and cedar trees of all shapes and sizes, decorated by civic groups for the annual Christmas tree challenge modeled after one in Durham, done Cedar Springs–style.

Spring thought of all the goodwill and positive emotions that filled the room at Christmastime. None of that was present today. To Spring's ears, the murmurs of those gathered and waiting for the proceedings to begin sounded hostile and on edge.

That's because the overall sentiment of those who had come for the meeting could best be described as suspicion. It was ten minutes to three and a good thirty people were already scated and waiting for the meeting to begin with more coming in the back door. Most of them, like Spring and the historical society members, well remembered the end run that had been done on another piece of property. Before anyone knew what was happening or could do anything about it, that development deal was signed, sealed and under construction with no public input on the matter. That would *not* be the case this time.

Lovie Darling selected a seat in the middle of the second row and greeted people as she passed them. Spring knew the position would give them eye contact with all the planning commissioners, as well as a good view of any speakers who addressed the panel.

"I thought the developer was supposed to be here," Lovie said.

"I did, too," she answered.

The table to the left of the ones where the commissioners sat was designated as the spot for those who would address the body. Two large but empty easels were positioned near the table.

That didn't bode well, Spring thought, knowing that the significance of those easels hadn't escaped her mother's attention. Their presence indicated that there would be plans or architectural renderings to display and show off. And those sorts of plans meant that proposals had been developed already.

She might have to make that phone call to the historical society's attorney, after all.

"I wouldn't put it past Bernadette to have signed a contract already," Georgina Lundsford, another local resident with a deep and abiding passion for historical preservation, hissed as she leaned forward. "She's probably a silent partner in the development company."

Spring pulled her phone out of her handbag, put it on vibrate and left it on her lap.

A few moments later, a side door off the room opened and three people entered. Spring stifled a gasp.

Not at Cameron Jackson, her soon to be brother-in-law, or at Gloria Reynolds, the city council clerk. The man with them, in a dark blue suit and tie, the man with a laptop bag hanging from one shoulder and a large artist's portfolio bag from the other, was the one who arrested her attention.

In Cedar Springs for *business* meetings.

"I'm an architect," he'd said.

She should have put the pieces together. The evidence had been right in front of her. But the context had been all wrong. That's why she'd missed what should have been clear.

"Spring, darling, what's wrong?" Lovie asked.

Spring glanced at her mother, then realized that she was gripping the edge of her chair so hard that her knuckles were white.

Concentrating on regulating her breathing, she nodded. "I'm fine, Mom."

She released the chair and clasped her hands together in her lap on top of the mobile phone.

She should have known that a man like David Camden was too good to be true. He was a loving father and a man of faith. He was the first man to capture her feminine attention in many years.

And he was here to destroy her family's home and legacy.

Chapter Six

David saw her the moment he turned around to assess the crowd the fire chief had described as "openly hostile" as they'd made their way to the meeting room.

He'd walked in with Fire Chief Cameron Jackson and with Gloria, the helpful clerk who'd arranged for his meetings and helped him set up the items from his large portfolio.

Dr. Spring Darling sat front and center, staring daggers at him. The expression was one he'd always considered hyperbole until he saw those daggers directed his way. He saw disgust, distrust and sadness in her eyes. Her look cut him in a way that might cause actual physical wounds.

He wanted to rush over, to tell her that everything would be all right. But he knew that was not and could not be the case—at least where Spring, her mother and her sisters were concerned.

The main thing David wanted to get across during his presentation was that he was not a developer, that Carolina Land Associates studied and made recommendations on land use. The architectural side of the firm came up with renderings that would later be used by development firms. It was up to governing bodies to decide whether to proceed with a development project or not.

It took him about twenty minutes to run through his presentation. He answered a few clarification questions from the commissioners and then the meeting was open to questions from the floor.

David heaved an internal sigh when he saw who rose.

"How often are your recommendations followed by said governing bodies?"

The query from the audience came from Dr. Spring Darling.

"State your name, please," the clerk said.

"Spring Darling, MD, and member of the Cedar Springs Historical Society, as you well know."

David felt that information was directed at him rather than the council clerk, who did well know who Spring was.

He knew the answer, of course. Those data represented one of the benchmarks on which his architectural and consultancy firm could base success. There were a few ways he could answer the question, but the most direct and honest was the best approach.

"Thank you for that question, Dr. Darling," he said, walking closer to the assembled residents, the digital pointer he'd used to highlight points on the renderings in his palm. "Carolina Land Associates has a strong track record of meeting client needs. Our most recent analysis of that very data shows a 95.8 percent rate of acceptance of our primary recommendations."

Before Spring could answer, an older woman next to her, who could only have been her mother, rose. She wore a peach-colored dress and had the same coloring, cheekbones and eyes as Spring. He knew he was looking at an older version of the doctor and could see exactly what the pretty pediatrician would look like in thirty years—an older, more mature but still beautiful woman. Right now though, he also saw something close to anger in the eyes of the older version of Spring Darling.

"So you're telling us, Mr. Camden, that your top recommendation for this project, the new urbanism community you're *preliminarily* calling The Township at Cedar Springs, is parcel two?"

David glanced back at the easels and used the pointer to pinpoint the parcel she referred to. "It's larger, at just about two hundred acres, and this parcel is ideal for a mixed-use development," he said. "It wouldn't require the easements or the purchase of any existing construction or property. As you can see, unlike parcel one or parcel three, it has little developed land and abuts a trail that could be expanded into a nature—"

"Didn't you say your condo, retail and business development project needs a minimum of three hundred and preferably three-hundred seventy-five acres?"

"Yes, but—"

Before he could finish, the woman next to Spring Darling's mother was on her feet.

"And you plan to steal those additional two hundred acres via eminent domain. And before you can ask, Gloria, my name is Georgina Lundsford, and you," she said, pointing a hand that trembled with rage at David, "can build it over my dead body."

"Point of order," one of the planning commissioners said. "Georgina, sit down before we have to call the cops to haul you out of here."

"Was that a threat?" Mrs. Lundsford said, making as if she was about to climb over the chair in front of her and do something about it.

Several in the audience apparently interpreted the words as such and rose to Mrs. Lundsford's defense.

"It's just these bully tactics that are giving Cedar Springs a bad name!" someone called from the back.

"You tell 'em, Ross!"

Mrs. Lundsford reached down, and David briefly wondered if she would straighten up with a .38 or .45 aimed at him.

David wisely retreated to the table, where he stood behind both it and a chair.

Chief Llewelyn apparently hadn't been joking about the possible need for Kevlar or other protective gear in the planning commission meeting. David had foolishly thought that mere hyperbole. While Spring Darling and her mother may have been wishing him ill, Georgina Lundsford might very well act on that anger.

A moment later, though, she started reading—at the top of her lungs—from a booklet she held. And it sounded a whole lot like the US Constitution.

He glanced at Spring. She was leaning across her mother and trying to get the Lundsford woman to sit down and stop hollering at him and the commissioners. David had been following the reports in the *Cedar Springs Gazette* with a modicum of skepticism, but now he discovered the newspaper's online accounts had failed to capture the animosity that existed about this proposal.

David didn't have a personal opinion one way or the other. His goal was to get the planning commission to approve the preliminary plans, which would pave the way for the city council to give Carolina Land Associates the contract to draw up detailed architectural renderings for whichever site the city deemed suitable for a mixed-use project of shops, restaurants, businesses, residences and entertainment venues.

As more rumbling and grumbling came forth, David got a pretty good idea of just how angry mob mentality led to violence.

The chair of the planning commission was on his feet and still arguing with the man who'd accused him of being a bully. Georgina Lundsford had reached the Fourth Amendment and was practically screeching about "the right of the people to be secure in their persons, houses, papers and effects, against unreasonable searches and seizures."

The ever-growing hubbub included voices shouting encouragement like "That's right!" and a chant that was building up over the words of the Constitution: "We're gonna sue. We're gonna sue."

A big voice suddenly boomed over the din.

"Why doesn't everybody just take a seat?"

Heads turned to see Police Chief Zachary Llewelyn come in from the back, two officers flanking him. The chief made his way toward the front of the room while the two cops stood on either side of the assembled residents, who slowly looked around. Many sat again with uncertain looks at the officers and the police chief.

David hadn't anticipated being glad to see the law, but he sure hoped the big police chief could control his town. Cedar Springs, North Carolina, was supposed to be a sleepy little suburban city populated by professionals who worked in the Research Triangle area and commuted home to serenity every evening. Its residents were supposed to be retirees who liked the small-town vibe with city amenities, those who preferred a more altruistic approach to life. Apparently, they were willing to defend that to the core.

"You all right over there, Mr. Camden?"

David nodded to the police chief.

"You all ought to be ashamed of yourselves," Llewelyn told the gathered assembly. "Mrs. Lundsford, I told you after the last city council meeting that if you disrupted another public meeting, you were going to be cited."

"But, Chief, he…"

The police chief held up a hand. "With all due respect to you, Mrs. Lundsford, you were warned. The fine is going to cost you seventy-five dollars. Please don't up that misdemeanor to a felony. I don't want to arrest you."

She huffed and sat down with her Constitution, clearly not happy.

"Dr. Darling?"

David watched as Spring looked up at the police chief.

"I know you and your family have a vested interest in these proceedings, but you're going to have to control your historical society members."

David watched her reaction to the rebuke and felt for her. Her expression didn't change, but he thought he detected weariness in her eyes.

"I don't want to or plan to step on anybody's First Amendment rights to speak," the police chief told her, "but it has to remain civil. Understood?"

Spring nodded. She rose, followed by her mother and Georgina Lundsford. Others in the row made way as the three passed. Then about a dozen others who had been scattered throughout the audience joined the trio.

One of the officers who'd come in with the chief trailed them out of the room. When the door closed behind them, David looked at the planning commissioners, whose faces reflected varying degrees of shock and dismay.

"Well," Chief Llewelyn said to the front panel.

"Looks like you'll be able to finish your meeting in peace."

He walked to the back of the room and took a seat. The other officer remained on guard at the side of the room, presumably to escort out any other troublemakers.

The chair of the commission cleared his throat, then looked at his colleagues. "Uh, are there any other questions from the floor?"

No one said a word.

"All right. Is there a motion to accept and approve the preliminary plans from Carolina Land Associates?"

The woman to his left raised her hand. "I make a motion to accept and approve the three parcels within the city of Cedar Springs presented by Carolina Land Associates and to send the proposal to the city council with our recommendation to approve Carolina Land Associates as the architect and land use company of record for a mixed-use development in Cedar Springs."

Within moments, the motion was seconded and unanimously approved. The chair called the meeting adjourned, and David stared at the three charts on the easels.

He'd won.

Then why, he wondered, did the victory feel so hollow?

* * *

In the hallway, Spring seethed. Not only had she been publicly chastised and embarrassed; David Camden had played her for a fool, not once but twice.

She wasn't sure which hurt the most.

That was a lie.

David's betrayal hurt more. She'd expected the planning commission meeting to be pro forma. She'd just wanted them, and therefore Mayor Bernadette Howell, to know that they were on notice with the Cedar Springs Historical Society that this battle would not be an easy one.

What she hadn't expected was to be blindsided by her emotions.

She'd made a connection with David Camden, a connection that he'd thoroughly exploited.

Her mother and Georgina went to see to Georgina's police citation. Spring had a good mind to call their attorney to see if that could be challenged, but as people began filing out of the multipurpose room, she realized the meeting had ended.

"What happened?" she asked the first person who approached—Ross Parsons, who'd jumped up to defend Georgina. He wasn't a historical society member, but he owned land adjacent to one of the three parcels. Like Spring, he saw what was coming down the road and didn't think it boded well.

The man shook his head. "Rubber-stamped to the council with a gift bow slapped on top."

Spring shook her head in disgust; she'd expected as much. "Figures."

She was about to go in search of her mother when someone called her name. She turned to find David Camden hurrying to catch up with her and the historical society members.

"I have nothing to say to you," she told him.

"Let me explain," David said.

"Explain? You lied to me."

"I did no such thing," David said.

"First, you let me believe you were homeless, and now," she said, gesturing toward his large portfolio, "you gave a lie of omission."

"Did I?" he asked, not bothering to mask the sarcastic tone of the inquiry. "Was that when I told you and the receptionist at the free clinic that I could pay for my son's care and that I had insurance? Or maybe it was at the hospital when you were so busy throwing facts and figures at me about Common Ground's community care projects? Is that when, Spring? I told you in the hospital's cafeteria that I wasn't homeless. But you had a notion in your head and decided not to hear me. And I told you I was an architect in the city for business. I didn't know I was required to tell my kid's doctor my entire life story with a résumé and reference letters."

For several awful moments she wordlessly stared as he walked her back through all their encounters.

He'd arrived at the community care clinic with Jeremy in his arms. She'd just assumed…

And when they were talking in the hospital cafeteria, he'd said they weren't homeless and was about to say something else when she'd been called to the emergency department to help with its short staffing. That was unusual enough to warrant her justified distraction from their conversation—a conversation they'd never finished.

Embarrassed, Spring glanced at the floor. "I've been…" she started, swallowed and then looked up to meet his gaze. She'd made a major error. Her judgment had been clouded by what was on the surface—maybe in an attempt to quell the almost immediate attraction she'd had toward him, an attraction that was overwhelming in its sheer being.

"I made some assumptions," she told him. "And that's something I shouldn't have done. I'm sorry, David."

He sighed, the anger seeming to drain from him as he shifted the laptop bag on his shoulder.

"I didn't mean to lose my temper with you," he said. He nodded toward the room they'd recently vacated. "I wasn't prepared for that type of reception."

"You should have been," snapped a woman who was standing nearby and clearly eavesdropping.

"It's all right, Mary," Spring said. "Why don't you go catch up with the others? I'm fine here."

"Are you sure, Dr. Spring?"

Spring assured her that she was. Then, with a dubious look at David, the woman nodded. "You holler if you need some backup."

"I will," Spring told her with a gentle smile. The woman departed, and so did the warmth in Spring's voice and demeanor.

She took a step back, putting distance between them. Her moment of contrition about her assumptions had ended, and the reality of the situation came crashing back on her. "Your mission is to destroy my house!"

She may have been mistaken about his financial solvency, but on this she was more than certain. David Camden's objective in Cedar Springs, North Carolina, was to destroy her home, the history and heritage of the six generations of Darlings who'd come before her.

"You're here to steal my land," she added.

He shook his head. "I'm here to give the city council recommendations on three proposed sites."

"One of which is the mayor's preferred location.

And, I might add, a location that goes straight through Darling land—land she is probably already finagling to snatch via eminent domain."

"You could extend to the city a right of way, easements."

Spring snorted. "A fat lot of good that will do when a four-lane thoroughfare is on one side and a twenty-four-hour burger-hangout-slash-fast-food-drive-through-slash-gas-station-slash-multiplex-theater is on the other."

David folded his arms and regarded her. His laugh held no humor. "You're one of them," he said.

"One of who?"

"One of those self-righteous do-gooders who like to do good for the unfortunate," he said, adding air quotes around the word *unfortunate*, "as long as the application of said services doesn't touch your backyard. In my field, we have a name for folks like you, NIMBY. That stands for—"

"I know what it stands for," Spring snapped. "And this isn't about my backyard. It's about preserving history. You don't know me. You don't know anything about me, so you can keep your little name-calling and stereotyping to yourself."

Had the ice in the air between them been real, her words could not have been colder.

"Why would you think that this wouldn't be important to me?"

"Spring, I never said it wasn't important to you. I have a job to do here. That task is to integrate design with function and present options to elected officials and city staff."

"Options? What options?"

"They are as varied as each of the properties," he said, hedging.

"And among those options can be recommend taking the whole thing to some other city?"

David sighed and ran a hand over his face. "This is getting us nowhere, Spring. I'd like the opportunity to show you what it is I do. I think there are some misconceptions about exactly what that is and what I'm in Cedar Springs for."

Spring was pretty sure she knew exactly what it was he did and what Mayor Howell had in mind for the city. But for the sake of peace, she was willing to go along with him. They were on opposite sides of this issue, and there was little he could do to sway her on the topic of development.

But if—*when!*—she was honest with herself, she just wanted to spend some time with him, even though she was so angry. Since she could hardly admit *that* to him, she used the one plausible rationale she had at her disposal. Despite the shield she'd erected around her heart, David

Camden had somehow wiggled in when she wasn't on guard.

She was thirty-five years old, a responsible and respected adult in a professional field. Long gone were the frivolous years when she could act on any whim like her youngest sister, Autumn.

Spring shook her head. Who was she kidding? She'd never been young and carefree. She was thirty when she was ten. Her grandmother always said Spring was an old soul who took after her grandmother's mother. But did being rooted mean she had to be boring, not willing to take a chance when happiness unexpectedly presented itself in her path?

She'd been in love once, and all it had gotten her was a broken heart and a disciplinary citation in her academic file. The last ten-plus years had been spent making up for that indiscretion, proving to herself that she was no longer that vulnerable and naive medical student she'd been when she'd fallen hard for Keith Henson. Keith. Just his name made her shudder.

"Well?"

Spring blinked. "Huh?"

"You've clearly been standing there debating all of the pros and cons. I've seen the arguments flash across your face," David said. "Instead of looking for ways to say no, let me show you that your fears are misplaced."

She doubted he would be able to accomplish that. But she nodded her assent.

"All right, David. Show me."

They took the discussion outside, where both could get some air away from the prying eyes of a few onlookers who clearly wondered if there would be any additional fireworks to view.

"You give him what for, Doc!" an elderly woman he'd seen in the meeting room called as he followed Spring.

Outside city hall, the sun was shining warm and bright, in stark contrast to the chilly atmosphere inside the building.

If he had been hoping to be led to a downtown café for a repeat of their amiable conversation over lattes like before, he'd been sadly mistaken. Spring walked no more than a few yards from the building's main entrance to a bench that was in a grassy parklike area fronting the building. People sat on other benches nearby, none close enough to overhear a conversation. An elderly couple tossed bread crumbs to birds at one; a young mother with a stroller watched a toddler run after a puppy on another. Across the way, an older black man sipped from a cup and watched people go by.

"My intent was not to upset you or anyone," he said without preamble.

He watched as Spring placed her purse on her lap and then clasped her hands on top of it reminiscent of the way his grandmother used to sit in church. All that was missing were the white gloves and little hat that matched her shoes.

On Spring, the pose looked as prim and proper as it did on his nana. But the curves on the woman sitting there waiting for him to explain himself were far from grandmotherly.

He suspected she'd taken the afternoon off from work to attend the meeting. She was dressed in a light blue linen wraparound dress, one of those numbers that women could dress up or down depending on the occasion, and heels. She'd paired the outfit with a simple small crucifix on a gold chain around her neck and minimal makeup. The look suited her—well put together and subtle though unmistakably expensive. Not for the first time he wondered why she didn't have a husband and children to dote on.

The competitive businessman in him—or, rather, the caveman, he mused—wondered why she didn't have a family to tend to rather than expending so much energy on history. But David knew he was as passionate about his work as Spring was about her family's land. And he'd seen firsthand her commitment to her patients.

The words should have come easy to him, but he struggled to explain his work to this woman who'd been there for him in the middle of the night, this woman who had shown compassion and care beyond the call of duty toward his son.

For reasons he was unwilling to delve into too deeply, what she thought mattered to him—a lot. And right now, what she assumed was that he was out to destroy her family's long-held homestead.

The land was private, so none of his team had been able to survey it. But the images from Google Earth had shown just a few buildings on the vast acreage, and most of them were centered near a large house. A rudimentary trail that connected with the property owned by the city had lots of potential for a nature way that could be a key selling point to those who wanted to live in the new community.

The words were all there in his head, but when he verbalized them, they sounded condescending to his ears.

"You don't understand," he said.

"I have an undergraduate degree in biology and a medical degree," she said. "I'm capable of understanding complex sentences."

Ouch.

The lady had a bite.

He sighed. Then he loosened his tie and leaned forward on the bench, dropping his hands between his legs.

"We—"

"You."

He glanced at her. Then decided to concede that point. "My firm identified areas that were best suited for a couple of small retail shops, with garden-style apartments and midpriced condos, residences that would appeal to empty nesters as well as young professionals. There would be businesses to support the residents who call the community home."

"We have that here," she said. "Look around. It's called downtown."

Spring pointed down Main Street which had the look of a village. With the exception of the bookends of city hall and the library, none of the thoroughfare's buildings were more than two stories high.

"Everything you're seeing is the product of a recently completed downtown renovation effort to bring people and businesses downtown," she said. "And as you've gathered—or already knew when you met me—my family has more than a passing interest in these plans. Plans, I should add, that were hatched from Mayor Howell's vendetta against my mother."

"Excuse me?"

Spring sighed. "That was probably an exaggeration, at least my sisters and I would like to believe it is."

"I feel like I've stumbled into a feud between the Hatfields and the McCoys."

"No blood has been shed…yet," she said. "But as you saw in the meeting, tempers tend to run high on this topic."

"Yes, of the 'not in my backyard' variety."

Spring shook her head. "It's more than that. Something happened between them, my mother and Bernadette Howell. Neither I nor any of my sisters have been able to suss out from Lovie what it was."

"You call your mother by her first name?"

Spring's eyes widened, and she gave him a look that could only be called incredulous. "Not to her face! She may be approaching sixty, but she's still our mom and therefore the boss."

He smiled. "You favor her."

Spring shook her head. "You mean I look just like her. Everybody says so. At least I know that if I still exercise, remain healthy and stay out of Sweetings—and away from my sister Summer's cheesecake and cooking—I'll look good when I reach her age."

"Spring, I don't want what just happened in there to come between us."

"Us? There is no us."

He reached for her hand and held tight when she would have pulled away.

"I thought we'd made a connection. At the hospital and at the coffeehouse."

"I thought so, too," she said, tugging her hand free from his grasp. "But that was before I found out just what your business is here in Cedar Springs."

David pinched his nose and sighed. "All right, Spring," he said. He reached into the breast pocket of his suit jacket and retrieved a card and a fountain pen.

He scrawled something on the back and handed it to her.

Spring stared at the drying ink and then raised her gaze to meet his.

"My number. In case you change your mind. Jeremy and my mom will be in town for another day before they head home. I'll be here for two more days after that."

With nothing else to say, he got up, retrieved his laptop bag and the large portfolio containing the preliminary renderings and walked away without a backward glance.

Chapter Seven

The day was pretty much a bust for Spring. In a surly mood, she wasn't up for the rehashing of the meeting that she knew would take place if she went home and saw her mother.

Living on the estate the sisters affectionately called The Compound within a stone's throw of her mother's house had its advantages at times. This was not one of them.

She thought about driving out to the farm-house. But all that would do was remind her of just how precarious a situation that property might be in if David and the mayor got what they wanted. The very notion depressed her.

She picked up her mobile and speed-dialed Winter, the sister she could count on to get her mind off land deals and medical trauma. Even as she waited for the call to connect, she thought of young Jeremy Camden. He was such a sweet little boy. Like his father, he'd managed to squiggle into her consciousness in ways that she didn't want to explore too deeply for fear of what that excavation might reveal.

"Hey, Doc Sis. I was just talking about you," Winter said by way of hello.

The greeting made Spring smile. She was Doc Sis. Autumn was Coach Sis and Summer had the title Perfect Miss from the second-eldest Darling daughter. The reference was to Summer's pageant days and her reign as Miss Cedar Springs.

"What are you doing?" Spring asked.

"Getting ready to cut into a slice of strawberry cheesecake."

Spring groaned. "You're at Sweetings?"

"Better than that," Winter said.

Spring knew what that meant. Winter was at Summer's place. And if Summer was baking, there had been some sort of trauma or drama related to the wedding planning. "How much is left?"

"I'll hide a slice for you."

She didn't have a shift at the Common Ground clinic today. Deciding that talking about Summer's wedding plans was preferable to thinking about David Camden's plans to turn her farmhouse and land into a condo development with convenience stores, she hung up with Winter and got up from the bench in City Hall Park.

Spring paused at the park bench where the elderly black man still sat. He'd placed the cup on the ground and watched as she approached.

"Hi, Sweet Willie," she said.

He bowed his head as if tipping a hat to her. "Afternoon, Doc. Heard I missed a good one in there."

Spring scrunched her face up as she sat next to him. "That's one word to describe it." She looked him over, trying to be subtle about the cursory exam but knowing he wasn't fooled. She opened her bag.

"Uh-uh, Doc. I don't need a handout and I gots plenty of them cards of yours for when I decide I need some doctoring." He tapped his forehead. "You done give me so many of 'em, I gots the address and the numbers memorized."

Then, as if to prove his words true, he rattled off the address of the Common Ground Free Clinic and both its main telephone number and her mobile number.

She smiled and closed the bag. "All right. You're on to my tricks."

He grinned, and Spring realized that for a homeless man, Sweet Willie was awfully grounded and seemed at peace. Other homeless men and women that she encountered at the clinic or on the street seemed to have a ready tale of woe to share with anyone who would listen.

Sweet Willie seemed, for lack of a better word, content.

She wondered if maybe not doing so much was the key to contentment. She'd been searching for it for a while, but that particular emotional state always seemed to elude her. So she'd thrust her mind and her body into patient care at the hospital and at the clinic and during the hours when she wasn't doing that, she worked to restore old buildings and educate people about the history of the city.

Maybe she needed to adopt Sweet Willie's model. Just sit on a park bench on a pretty day and watch the world go by.

She regarded the man. "Would you at least let me give you a ride somewhere?"

He shook his head. "No, ma'am. I'm right where I need to be."

She patted his back and rose. "All right, then. You have yourself a good rest of the day."

"You, too, Doc."

Sweet Willie was still on her mind when she arrived at Summer's. She parked on the street in front of the house rather than block Winter in the driveway.

At the door, she girded herself for the happy discussion that would take place inside. The thought of it gave her a pang, and she almost turned around to head back downtown where she knew she could sit in companionable silence with Sweet Willie.

"Stop being ridiculous, Spring," she said.

"Who are you talking to?"

She hadn't even heard the door open, yet there stood Summer in shorts and a scoop-neck top looking like a model for a designer's casual-elegant line of sportswear, while Spring thought she herself looked positively matronly in the plain wrap dress she'd worn to work that morning in anticipation of the afternoon meeting at city hall. The shoes were the only concession she'd made, but they had remained in the car until she'd arrived at city hall, where she'd met up with her mother and Mrs. Lundsford.

Spring shook her head. "Just muttering to myself," she said, entering. She kicked off her shoes in the foyer and dropped her handbag on a table just inside the door.

Summer trailed behind her toward the parlor where they usually gathered.

"It took you long enough," Winter said. "I had to fight them off to save a slice for you."

"After the day I've had, I think I need more than a single slice of cheesecake," Spring said.

Winter handed over the plate, and Summer chuckled. "I guess that's my cue to make espresso."

"Make it a double shot," Spring said.

"How can you sleep with that stuff in your system?"

"I built up an immunity while doing my residency. It's never worn off," Spring said, sinking her fork into the tip of the slice of cheesecake. "What's up with this?" she said lifting the plate.

They all knew that Summer only baked when she was stressed out.

Winter leaned back to make sure their younger sister was out of earshot.

"The wedding," Winter reported. "Summer wants a small affair, just family and close friends."

"And Cameron wants a royal to-do?"

Winter shook her head. "He wants whatever will make Summer happy and would just as soon have Reverend Graham marry them right here in the kitchen with the mailman and the trash collector as witnesses than go through with a big wedding that's starting to make her miserable."

"So, what's the problem?"

"Your mother and his mother," Summer said, reentering the parlor. "I knew you'd blab just as soon as my back was turned," she told Winter.

For her part, Winter didn't look repentant. "It wasn't blabbing. It was keeping Spring nformed."

Summer handed Spring the little espresso cup

and a coaster, then plopped into the chair facing the sofa where her sisters sat.

"What about me?" Winter complained.

"Blabbers can make their own coffee," Summer intoned.

Shaking her head, Winter rose. "I get no respect."

"And deserve none," Summer shot back.

Spring smiled at the bantering. Some things never changed no matter how old they were.

"Where's our merry fourth?" she asked of their youngest sister.

"Autumn has a game at the rec center tonight," Summer said. "Don't ask me which sweaty sport it is because I have not the first idea."

"It's a soccer clinic," Winter hollered from the kitchen, from where there suddenly came sounds of much clanging and swooshing.

"How can she hear over all that racket?" Summer whispered to Spring.

"I heard that!" came from the voice from the kitchen.

Summer's blue eyes widened, and she cast a glance toward the kitchen.

Spring laughed and shook her head. One of these days it would dawn on Summer that she always asked the same question about Winter's hearing, and, knowing her sister, Winter could always anticipate Summer's next question to whomever was nearby. She didn't have to actually hear it to know Summer would ask.

After taking a sip of the espresso, Spring placed the little cup on the coaster on the end table. "What's going on with Mom and Cameron's mother?"

Summer sighed. "Lovie got it into her head that it would be just lovely to have the wedding at the country club and mentioned that to Carol, who just adored the idea of her son getting hitched at a country club."

"It's your wedding. The bride gets to decide."

Summer gave her a look, and Spring knew her sister was right. Once Lovie Darling got her mind wrapped around an idea, it was hard to let it go.

Winter returned with a cup of tea in one hand and a Diet Coke in the other. "If I were evil like you, I'd just toss the can your way," she told Summer, handing her the soft drink.

"What was all that racket if you were making tea?"

"I was trying to use your fancy machine," Winter said.

"Guess it'll have to go to the repair shop now," Summer intoned. The comment earned another grin from Spring.

"Love you, too," Winter said, settling back on the sofa.

"We're thinking about eloping."

That earned Summer raised eyebrows from both sisters.

"Oh my," Winter eventually said.

"I know, I know," Summer said. "Lovie will have a cow. But I've had a big wedding before. And Cameron just wants to get married without all the hoopla."

"Then do it," Spring advised.

Summer tucked a foot under her on the chair and bit her bottom lip, then pulled a tube of lip gloss from her shorts pocket and applied it to her mouth. "It feels wrong," she said. "Like cheating."

With the elopement avenue closed, Spring asked, "Have you given either of the mothers a date?"

She nodded. "Next spring. In May. I like that month. The early flowers are in bloom."

"Mom isn't paying for anything, is she?" The question, which Spring had just been about to ask, came from Winter.

"Goodness, no," Summer said. "She and Daddy gave me a wedding already. I wouldn't hear of it. The engagement party is the conces-sion-slash-compromise," she said with air quotes, "that we made on that score."

Spring bit back a sigh. The engagement

party. This was the last thing she'd wanted to talk about.

"You know," Summer said, "I wouldn't be in this bind with her if one of you would bother to find a decent guy to marry."

"Operative word being *decent*," Winter said. "My last date was a disaster."

"When'd you go on a date?"

Winter stuck her tongue out at Summer in answer to the question.

"He was a decent enough guy," Spring said. "He just turned rotten when he forgot to tell you about the criminal convictions."

"What?" Summer squeaked. "Why don't I know this? What happened? Who is he?"

Spring reached for her espresso. Winter sipped her tea and then calmly said, "How many are on the guest list for the engagement party?"

Not so easily put off by the tactic, Summer narrowed her eyes at her sisters. "I want to know what's going on."

"Nothing," Winter said. "That's the point. Now, back to your little soiree."

Summer sighed. "At the rate you-know-who is going, we'll need to rent the country club for the engagement party."

"I thought it was supposed to be at The Compound," Winter said.

"It is. In the garden. You know, a nice little

backyard garden party. How are you two coming along on dates, by the way? It'll be so much better if all four of us have some eye candy on the arm."

"Eye candy? Since when do you talk like that?"

Summer blushed. "I heard someone at Manna say that. She was talking about a couple of the firefighters who have been volunteering there."

"Uh-huh," Winter said.

Spring had already made her position on this known on two previous occasions and had no intention of changing her mind. The last thing she needed was some hapless man getting the wrong idea about her interest in him by inviting him to escort her to a family affair like an engagement party. She'd already run through a mental list of potential doctors and staffers at the hospital, and every single one of them would come to the wrong conclusion about such an invitation. The rest of her social acquaintances were married or nonexistent.

She could, of course, ask Sweet Willie to escort her. The fact of the matter was she felt far more comfortable with him than with someone who might be considered more socially acceptable. The leech she'd almost married years ago had the sort of pedigree that would appeal to most women. He'd said and done all the right things to woo her and sweep her off her feet. What he lacked was human decency or a conscience. He was after one thing, and Spring's heart was not it. The only good thing that had come of the debacle was that vows had not been exchanged between them.

"Spring?"

She blinked and focused on her sisters. "Yes?"

"You weren't listening to a word I said," Summer accused.

"Guilty as charged," Spring said. "I was thinking about—"

"Oh, my goodness!" Summer exclaimed. "Today was the planning commission meeting. I totally forgot. How did it go?"

From one topic she didn't want to talk about straight into another.

Spring sighed and resigned herself to rehashing the fiasco that had been the meeting—leaving out the parts about her private interactions with David Camden.

"Are you sure you want to do business with these people?" Charlotte Camden asked her son after he summarized his day with the officials and residents of Cedar Springs.

Because Jeremy was sleeping, they'd opted for dinner in David's room while Jeremy lay sprawled across the second bed in Charlotte's room. They'd ordered their meals and sat talking while waiting for them to be delivered. But after they said grace, David found that his appetite wasn't quite what he'd thought it would be.

He poured vinaigrette on his salad, then put the cruet on the table with a weariness that was bone deep.

"I don't have to like the people I work with or for."

"It helps," Charlotte said. "The police chief really threatened to arrest them all?"

"For all intents and purposes. Of course we've encountered opposition before. This just..." He shook his head.

"I know you care for her."

"Who?"

"David," Charlotte said with the tone he'd learned from her and sometimes used with Jeremy. "Do not insult my intelligence."

He sighed. "Nothing about this trip has been what I anticipated," he said. "I'm questioning if this was the right move for the company."

Charlotte reached across the table for his hand. "What's already in motion is in motion, dear. If this isn't where the Lord wants you, He'll direct you to some other place. Trust in Him, David."

He stabbed a piece of lettuce with his fork. Instead of eating it, he poked around on the plate as if digging for a rare vegetable.

"I'm trying to, Mom. I'm trying."

"Daddy."

David and Charlotte looked toward the open door of the adjoining room. Jeremy stood there in the new pair of Winnie the Pooh pajamas that David had picked up for him the day after the appendectomy. Jeremy had the teddy bear Beau with him. The two had been pretty much inseparable from the moment Jeremy claimed him from his "most favorite doctor in the whole wide world." When he went to the bathroom, so did Beau. And when he got tucked into bed, so did the bear.

David went to his son and scooped him up in his arms. "Hey, buddy. What are you doing up?" In answer, Jeremy leaned his head on his father's shoulder, but held on to the teddy bear by its ear. "How's that tummy feeling? Okay?"

The boy nodded.

"Would you like something to eat, darling?" Charlotte asked.

Jeremy shook his head and burrowed even closer to David.

"Beau wants some banana."

David glanced at his mother. "Does he now? Well, let's see about getting him some. Okay?"

Jeremy nodded.

David settled them on the sofa while Charlotte got and peeled half of one of the bananas on the desk. He placed his palm on his son's forehead, feeling for a temperature. Jeremy seemed a little groggy and unusually clingy, but that was pretty much to be expected after his surgery.

Charlotte came and sat on the edge of the sofa with a few slices of banana on a small plate. "Here you go, sweetness," she said, handing Jeremy a piece of the fruit.

He nibbled on it without much enthusiasm.

"You should finish your dinner, Mom."

She returned to the table while Jeremy offered some of his banana to his teddy bear.

"Why don't you eat that?" David said. He patted Beau's stomach. "He looks pretty full to me, but this little tummy has a ways to go," he said, patting Jeremy's.

That earned him a tiny smile.

"Daddy?"

"Yeah, buddy?"

"I want Dr. Spring."

David wanted to say, *So do I, buddy. So do I. But we can't always get what we want.*

Instead, he glanced up at his mother, who raised an eyebrow in anticipation of his response.

David didn't have one that would satisfy either of them.

Chapter Eight

The next day Spring and her best friend Cecelia Jeffries met up with the other historical society members at the Corner Café downtown. The blowup during the meeting the previous day had been a setback but by no means the end of the issue. Nothing would be built overnight, and, unless the city council called a special meeting, its next one wasn't scheduled for a couple of weeks. So they had a little bit of time before things got truly critical. Their mission now was to determine a strategy to get Mayor Howell to be reasonable in the plans for the new mixed-use development.

"I'm not sure that the words *reasonable* and *Bernadette Howell* belong in the same sentence," Cecelia said as she perused the day's specials on the big chalkboard.

"She keeps saying that this land use firm is

only doing preliminary work in order to make recommendations for development sites," Spring said. "But I don't buy it."

"Well," Gerald intoned, "there's ample reason to suspect what she says because it rarely matches what she does. You all do remember what happened the last time she said something was in the quote-unquote *preliminary* stage."

"The Junction at Commerce Plaza," several in the small group said with a unified groan. A moment of silence ensued as if each person needed to mourn for a moment the fiasco of that development project.

The Junction was a twenty-four-hour multi-bay gas and service station, convenience store and car wash that put an incredible strain on what had been a green out parcel of Commerce Plaza. The city had to, at considerable unbudgeted taxpayer expense, add two north–south turn lanes, a traffic light system and curb and gutter just to deal with the increased vehicular traffic. The site had been cleared and paved with foundation before the historical review committee could get an injunction on any of the work for, among other things, an archaeological dig of the area. A judge ultimately ruled that it would have been more detrimental to the city to undo the work or to cancel the contracts that had already been approved.

The group wanted to ensure that the mayor's latest pet project didn't turn into the Junction 2.0.

"What do you think of as gourmet food when you think of Poland?" Georgina Lundsford asked, apparently talking to no one in particular as she waited in line.

"What?" Cecelia asked.

"Just like the mayor and being reasonable don't go together, neither does Poland and gourmet food." Gerald turned to face Georgina from his position in line to order lunch. "Don't get me wrong," he said, taking her odd comment at face value. "There is a wonderful cuisine out of the country, but the label 'gourmet'?" He shrugged. "I don't think so. There are a lot of comfort foods in Polish cuisine. Lots of sausage and sauerkraut and several types of breads."

"Looks like someone didn't take her medication again this morning," Cecelia whispered to Spring.

The two exchanged an amused glance. Get this group started on the topic of food, and they might never get around to the real business at hand.

"And pierogis," Georgina said, linking her arm with Gerald's. "Those are yummy. I wish they had some here. Maybe I'll make some for dinner next week. What did you decide, Gerald, dear? Do you want one of these soups?"

"I'm all for comfort food," he said. "Since the burglary at the shop, that's all I can seem to manage."

Georgina patted his arm. "It was such a sad day," she said. "But the good thing is that although you and Richard had things stolen from Step Back in Time Antiques, neither of you was physically harmed. Insurance will take care of the rest."

"Have the police arrested anyone yet?" Spring asked Gerald.

"No, but they assure us that they're following several leads." With another look at the menu boards, he said, "C.J. makes a pretty mean baked macaroni and cheese. I think that's what I'll have."

"Really?" Georgina asked, sounding equally mystified and horrified. "Didn't you say that's what you had for dinner last night?"

Gerald winked at her. "That's right. I did. You ladies drown yourselves in Häagen-Dazs when you're upset. For me, it's mac and cheese."

That earned him a laugh from the group. After placing their assorted orders for sandwiches, soups and other lunch items, the Cedar Springs Historical Society members claimed several tables near the back of the dining room. Pushing them together, they made one communal table for the entire bunch. After everyone got settled with sweet tea, coffee or sparkling water, Spring got down to business.

"We have to do something," she said, reaching back to dig into the tote bag she'd put over the back of her chair. She pulled out a small leather portfolio and plucked several pages from it. "This is the only one they had at the library. I took the liberty of making several copies."

She handed them around to her friends.

Georgina squinted at the small writing, which was a photocopy of a photocopy. "I have trouble if there are too many things to follow," she said. "Where are my glasses?" Gerald lifted them from her head and handed them to her. She offered him a smile in thanks. "This is from a database, right, Spring?"

"Yes," she said. "I'll read it back to you."

She then provided the highlights of all the information she'd gleaned. When she finished, the entire group looked glum. The old property records just muddied the waters. While the Darling land ownership wasn't in question and never had been, some other parcels had dubious title due to several "gentlemen's agreements" made in the 1930s and 1940s regarding property lines.

"You know," Georgina said. "Maybe instead of trying this tactic, we should do something else."

"Like what?" Cecelia asked. "The only other thing I can think of is an outright intervention."

Spring looked thoughtful for a moment, then said, "Hmm."

"No, Spring," Cecelia intoned.

"It could work," Spring said. "An intervention might not be such a bad idea."

"I was joking," Cecelia said, casting a worried glance around the table. "It was a joke, Spring."

The historical society's president nodded. "But it doesn't have to be."

The more Spring thought about it, the more the idea appealed to her. But what she had in mind wasn't an intervention for the mayor. Bernadette Howell's mind would not be swayed no matter how convincing the arguments or how rational the case the Cedar Springs Historical Society made.

No, what Spring realized is that David Camden needed to see firsthand what was at stake. He needed to know and understand that it was more than her family's desire to make things difficult, a perspective the mayor held. He needed to see that the society's opposition was not because her family wanted to lord their wealth over everyone else, a supposition put forth by at least one pro-development resident in a letter to the editor of the *Cedar Springs Gazette*.

The Darlings were not opposed to progress. The family's lasting legacy to the city of Cedar Springs was that it had the resources it needed to thrive…and it had, growing from an enclave of farming families into a bustling village and from there a thriving city that was a suburban hideaway for those who liked the proximity and amenities associated with an urban area without all the attendant crime, blight and malaise.

Spring wasn't naive. Cedar Springs had its share of problems, the creep of crime from Raleigh and Durham to the north and up from Fayetteville to the south seemed to be growing rather than decreasing. And homelessness was an ongoing problem. But that didn't mean that she or the historical society had to abandon hope or succumb to pressure to make Cedar Springs a cookie-cutter facsimile of every other municipality in North Carolina.

She didn't want to drag all the historical society members into the mix. The idea she had for David needed to be confined to an intimate group. And Spring knew just which group could and would want to be a part of her little intervention. This was a plan that could be carried out by the Magnolia Supper Club. So Spring let the rest of the meeting at the Corner Café swirl on around her.

Georgina Lundsford proposed a rally in the town square outside city hall and the public administration building. Gerald suggested posters, à la "Save Cedar Springs," that could be printed up and placed in front of store windows or on bulletin boards and staked in front yards of like-minded residents. And Millicent Graves, bless her heart, who still wore her hair long and plaited like she had during the 1960s protest movements, offered as a plan a sit-in and march to make the city's elected officials see reason.

Spring's phone vibrated in her pocket. She pulled it out, expecting to see a message from the hospital or the clinic. It was instead a text message from Cecelia, who was sitting directly across from her at the table.

Does she know that it's not 1968?

Spring bit back a smile and tapped a quick reply.

Don't worry. I have another idea.

Cecelia lifted her brows in silent query to Spring, who shook her head ever so slightly. "Later," she mouthed.

With a nod, Cecilia reached for a pita chip from the large bowl of complimentary snacks being shared by the table.

A little more than an hour after the group dispersed, with marching orders to bring viable action ideas to the next meeting, Spring outlined her idea to Cecelia.

"Spring, I'm not sure this is such a good idea," Cecelia said.

Spring was behind the wheel of her Volvo car with Cecelia riding shotgun as they made their way to the Darling farmhouse. On the southern outskirts of town, the property known by locals as the Darling Homestead was now a mere fraction of the more than ten thousand acres it had been when the first Darling settled the property. Much of the city of Cedar Springs had originally been Darling land. What remained today was mostly undeveloped former farmland. The property included a rambling farmhouse that generations of Darlings had grown up in, a barn and silo, former stables and several unused outbuildings that had once been storage facilities or way-station cabins for farmhands to shelter in during storms.

Spring wanted to take a quick inventory and see what, if anything, would need to be done for the house to be in shape for a dinner party. Her mother had a service out every couple of weeks to dust and tend to the grass. Since she'd returned home to Cedar Springs from Georgia, Spring's younger sister Summer went to the farm frequently to garden and to enjoy the quiet. Summer had restored the extensive gardens that once were carefully tended by their grandmothers. For all four Darling sisters, Spring, Summer, Winter and Autumn, the house in the country was a refuge, but for Summer it seemed to be even more than that. She'd come out, worked the garden and its flowers and sat on the front porch swing sipping lemonade as she'd worked through her relationship with Cameron Jackson.

For Spring, the history of the property and her family's legacy and contribution to that history mattered even more.

"It's so peaceful out here," Cecelia said. "I always feel the stress just seeping away whenever I visit."

"That's why we love it," Spring said. "You know you're welcome to use the house whenever you want to get away."

"Your mother has been trying to give me a key for years now."

"You should take her up on it," Spring said. She added a beat later, "Before it's too late. As a matter of fact, there's an extra in the kitchen at the house. I'll give it to you today."

As they drove, the terrain drifted almost imperceptibly from business to residential and then to tree-lined two-lane road. The trees gave way to open fields strewn with wild flowers on one side and an apple orchard on the other.

"Take it all in," Spring said. "The orchard

owner sold his parcels to the city six months ago. I made a counteroffer, a generous one, too."

"You're kidding," Cecelia said. "You never said anything."

Spring shook her head and swerved around a strip of tire rubber on the roadway.

"It all happened so fast," she said. "You know how things work here. The girls even offered me their own money to increase the bid. But the city, via the economic development office, made him an offer he said he couldn't refuse."

"That's just wrong."

"But it's how the game is played," Spring said, "And from what I discovered in my research, I think he knew some of his land probably fell under one of those not quite clear titles. If the city was willing to pay him and sort out the titles, he was willing to take the cash and run."

She pointed out the front windshield, adding, "This land abuts ours, so that's how and when I knew the mayor or someone at city hall had a hand in the play that was in motion. Ross Parsons's property abuts another small, now city-owned, property. Mayor Howell says the land-use consultant is surveying several sites, but mark my words, if David's plans go forward, everything you're seeing right now will be paved over. That will be asphalt instead of apple trees, and that barn over there," she said, indicating a picturesque red barn with horses grazing nearby, "will be a big-box retailer open twenty-four hours a day and offering every imaginable convenience known and unneeded by man."

Cecelia chuckled, a deep, throaty sound of amusement. "Your pioneer roots are showing."

Spring glanced over at her and grinned. "They can't be," she said. "I just had a touch-up."

"Ha! I knew those blond—"

"CeCe, look," Spring interrupted and pointed out the front window.

Cecelia's gaze followed the direction of Spring's hand.

In the middle of the road, a good fifty yards in front of them, was a man. Although the day was fairly warm, he had on a long duster jacket reminiscent of something from the Old West.

"I think that's Sweet Willie up there," Cecelia said.

"Willie?" Spring said. "From Manna?"

She knew he was partial to her sister Summer's cooking and always complimented her on the meals at Manna, the soup kitchen operated by the Common Ground ministries, whether it was a simple turkey sandwich on wheat bread or more elaborate fare.

"What is he doing way out here by himself?" Cecelia asked.

"The better question," Spring said, "is *how* did

he get out here? We're a good twenty miles from downtown. Surely he didn't walk."

Since neither woman had an answer readily available, Spring continued driving toward him, closing the distance between them in a manner of moments.

He'd turned at the sound of the car and shuffled to the side of the road.

"I have a first-aid kit in the trunk," Spring said. "I hope he's not injured. He's such a sweet man."

The man known as Sweet Willie stood at the side of the road. A scowl marred his pecan-brown features; the mouth that was usually turned up in a smile of welcome didn't seem at all pleased to see them.

"What is he up to?" Spring said.

Cecelia glanced at her. "Why does he have to be up to something? Because he's a black man on a country road?"

Spring heard a note of defensiveness in her friend's voice. "I didn't mean anything by it, Cecelia. I'd ask the same question of anyone out on this road, black, white or otherwise."

"I know," Cecelia said, conceding the point. "There's just something off about him."

"What do you mean?" Spring asked as they drew up alongside the man, who was suddenly smiling from car to ear.

"Like there's another layer or layers to him," Cecelia said as Spring put the car in Park. "It's just a vibe I get," she added. "He's very well-spoken."

"Now who is doing the stereotyping?" Spring asked. "An elderly black and homeless man can't be well-spoken? And are we talking about the same Sweet Willie? When I talk to him, he sounds like an older man, someone who came of age in a time when things were different."

"That's just it," Cecelia said, slipping on sun-glasses. "I don't think he's as elderly as he lets people assume."

By the time they got out of the car, Sweet Willie looked the way he usually looked, of an inde-terminate but advanced age, slightly stooped and bearing the smile that warmed so many hearts at Manna, the Common Ground soup kitchen.

"Well, look at what the good Lord has sent my way," he said. "Two pretty ladies to rescue me in my time of need."

"Sweet Willie," Spring said, giving him as thorough a once-over as she could—for the sec-ond time in two days. She was relieved to see that he suffered no visible wounds or distress. "What in the world are you doing so far out here in the country?"

"The country is a good place to think, Doc,"

he said. Then, with a nod acknowledging Cecelia, he added, "Dr. Jeffries."

The tall black woman nodded but didn't say anything, her inscrutable expression hard to read. Spring thought it contained more than a smidgen of suspicion. She wondered about her friend's reaction to the homeless man. Cecelia was a fairly decent judge of character, so her suspicion of and response to Willie were fairly disconcerting.

"Can we give you a ride back into town?" Spring asked.

Willie's gaze left hers and focused on something over Spring's shoulder. She turned to see what had captured his attention.

A motorcycle driver was headed down the road, the lone figure a dark blur at the moment. She turned back to face Willie, concerned about the elderly man.

"It's a nice day for a ride," Willie said, watching intently as the biker approached and then passed them.

Spring and Cecelia shared a glance. Spring held out her arm, directing him toward the car. "Come on," she said. "We can drop you off wherever you'd like."

With a final glance toward the disappearing motorcyclist, the man let them lead him to the car, where Spring got him settled and buckled into the front seat while Cecelia slipped into the backseat.

Their conversation back into town was short. Willie fell asleep almost as soon as the car started moving. His head lolled against the window, and he issued periodic snorts and snuffles.

"He was wide-awake not five minutes ago," Cecelia said from the backseat.

"I hope he's all right," Spring said. "I wonder when he last had a physical checkup. I wish he'd come to the clinic for an assessment. Hand me my purse, will you?"

"Not while you're driving," Cecelia said.

Spring met her friend's gaze in the rearview mirror and shook her head. "Between you and Summer, you could do a commercial for the DMV about distracted driving. Every time I turn around she's telling someone, 'No texting and driving.' As if I text a lot."

"Autumn does and can be a bit reckless," Cecelia pointed out.

"True," Spring agreed of her youngest sister.

"You still up to going out to the house with me after we get Willie settled?"

Cecelia glanced at her watch. "Sure. I have some papers to read, the thesis outlines for a couple of my grad students. But I'm good. Let's get those leaves in the table and see what else you might need for this ill-advised dinner."

Because he hadn't stated a destination, Spring drove to the Common Ground homeless shelter. She parked in front and turned toward him. "Willie? We're here."

Cecelia passed Spring's handbag up to her.

When there was no response from the sleeping man, Spring gently shook him awake. "Willie?"

"Huh? What?" the man said, rustling into a sitting position. He looked around as if not sure where he was.

"We're at the shelter. Is that all right?"

He smiled. "Oh, thank you, Dr. Darling. I was dreaming I went up to the Pearly Gates and the good Lord had two beautiful attendants there to greet me. One was tall and blonde and pretty and the other was tall and dark and had a voice that sounded like honey and molasses."

Spring laughed as she pulled a bill and a small card from her wallet. "I'm sure it'll be a while before you're ready to meet Gabriel or anyone else at the Pearly Gates. You do have to stay healthy and well, though. You know, you can always stop by the Common Ground clinic anytime for a free checkup just to make sure everything's okay."

"So you told me yesterday, Doc. The good Lord willing," he said as he struggled to undo the seat belt, "these old bones will keep moving for a while."

"Let me get that," Spring offered, reaching

to unclasp the seat belt mechanism. "Everyone always has trouble with it."

"Much obliged," he said. "For the ride and your kindness. Both of you."

With the clasp loose, he reached for the door handle, but Spring halted him with a gentle hand on his arm. "Will you take this?" she said. "It's just a little something and the card has my number on it if you ever need anything or want to come in for that health assessment."

He looked down at the twenty-dollar bill she offered. Willie smiled. "You keep giving me them cards. Keep your money, Dr. Darling. There's others out here who need it more than me."

"Please," she said.

He plucked the business card from her hand but left the currency. "Much obliged again for your kindness."

He was then out of the car with an agility that seemed incongruous with the rest of him.

As Cecelia moved from the backseat to the front, they watched him. Instead of heading into the shelter, he loped off and turned onto a side street. When Cecelia shut the door, she faced Spring.

"What homeless person turns down a free twenty?"

Spring started the car. "I don't know," she said. "He has a lot of pride."

"He has a lot of something," Cecelia said. "He's awfully spry for an old man. And those boots were not your run-of-the-mill discount-store type. Those were expensive."

"When did you have time to study his footwear?" Spring asked. "Which could easily have been picked up at a clothes closet."

"I doubt it," Cecelia said. "And I noticed when he got in the car. I'm very observant, you know."

"So you've told me," Spring said on a dry note.

"Scoff if you want," Cecelia insisted. "But there's something not as it should be about that man. I still say there's something under the surface."

"What?" Spring asked before putting on the turn signal and pulling into traffic. "You think he's *pretending* to be homeless?"

Cecelia's brow furrowed. "I don't know. I do know one thing for sure."

"What's that?"

"He was pretending to be asleep. He was wide-awake and heard everything we said."

"Well, it's a good thing we didn't say anything bad," Spring said. "And what makes you think he wasn't really asleep?"

"I'm a college professor," Cecelia said. "I know when people are asleep for real."

"Experience with those grad students who sleep through your esoteric lectures, huh?"

"Ha-ha," Cecelia replied in ill humor.

"Aren't you Miss Rosy Sunshine today."

Cecelia folded her arms with a "Humph." When Spring just chuckled, she added, "I'm telling you—Sweet Willie is hiding something. He never answered the question of why he was out there and just conveniently fell asleep. I think it was so he wouldn't have to tell us what he was doing just walking along a country road."

Although she was hesitant to admit it, the same thing had bothered Spring.

What was he doing out there wandering around? There was nothing to see or do that far outside the downtown or Commerce Plaza districts. But she wasn't going to give credence to the seed of Cecelia's conspiracy theory. Despite having earned multiple doctorate degrees and being a preeminent scholar at Duke University, Cecelia had a tendency to make connections where there were none to be made.

So instead of addressing that topic, she responded to an earlier comment her friend had made. "Why do you think the dinner party is ill-advised?"

"It's not the dinner or the party part that I'm concerned about," Cecelia said. "It's your plan to ambush David Camden there that has me worried."

* * *

The man known as Sweet Willie watched as the Volvo car continued down the street, the two women talking as they drove and unaware of his scrutiny. After the car made a turn, presumably to head back out to the Darling property off Orchard Road, he pulled out a mobile phone and stepped farther back into the side street where he'd ducked to get out of their line of sight.

He punched in the familiar phone number and skipped the pleasantries when the connection was made.

"I couldn't make the meeting," he said, without the slow and polite drawl of a Southern gentleman of a certain age. "A couple of the city's resident do-gooders saw me on Orchard Road. They know me as Sweet Willie, and I couldn't chance arousing their suspicions any more than they are."

He listened for a moment as he glanced around to make sure no one was nearby; then he nodded. "Yeah. I saw him. Luckily he accurately assessed the situation and kept rolling… Nope, there's no way they saw his face. He was just a guy on a motorcycle taking the scenic route. He didn't even slow down. I barely managed to get out of an explanation on what I was doing out there," he told the person on the other end. "If a biker had stopped to chitchat, there'd be no way to explain that."

"Yeah, I know. Time's running out. The Elmhurst Street situation is getting dire. We're going to have to make a move to get both operations… Yeah, even though we don't know that."

He listened for a bit, then said, "Tell him to get what he can. I'll need to come up with another meet site. We can't risk getting caught out there again."

He pocketed the phone and glanced each way before making his way back out and onto the main street.

The man assumed the lope-shuffle of Sweet Willie and ambled along his way.

Chapter Nine

Spring felt a pang of guilt but knew that what she was about to do was for the good of a greater cause. She kept telling herself that and hoped that she would believe it...eventually.

She stared at the number David had put on the back of his business card and dialed it before she changed her mind.

It was a good plan. Nothing would go awry. It was actually the ideal way to do what needed to be done.

When David answered, she took a deep breath and plunged into the deep end.

"I'm so glad you called," he said. "Jeremy has been asking for you."

Immediately thoughts of subterfuge left her mind. "Is he all right? Where are you? Has he had some sort of setback? Do you need to get him back to the hospital? I can meet you there."

David's chuckle rumbled through the line, and Spring liked the sound of it.

"Calm down, Doc," he said. "He's fine. He and Beau wanted to see you."

"Oh."

Spring's heart suddenly beat a little faster than it had been mere moments ago. But this was for a different cause. She thought she heard more in what he'd said than the words that came through the wireless receiver.

"And I did, too," David added a second later.

She placed a hand over her heart, whether to feel it beating or to calm it down she couldn't determine.

"David…"

"We're still at the hotel. My mother will take him home tomorrow."

"I'd like to see…him."

You.

"We're in Rooms 148 and 150."

"I'm on my way."

Madness, that's what this is, Spring thought fifteen minutes later as she made her way down the carpeted hall of the hotel toward the rooms inhabited by the Camden family. She could and should turn around and head to a saner locale.

But she was a doctor, and a patient needed a house call.

"Whatever you have to tell yourself," she muttered as she knocked on the door to Room 148.

She hadn't even thought to bring her emergency medical bag with her. It was tucked in her trunk with other essentials like galoshes, for stomping around the areas at the farm that had vernal pools, and collapsible crates often needed to haul things from estate sales and historic sites being restored. Also apparently locked in the trunk of her car was her good sense. She'd been born with a lot of it, but she had lost it the moment she met David and Jeremy Camden.

Spring was about to turn and run when the hotel room door opened and Charlotte Camden greeted her.

"Dr. Darling! I'm so glad you could stop by. Jeremy is going to be thrilled to see you again. He's been asking about you. Come on in."

Charlotte wore a flowing silk paisley caftan and was a gracious hostess in their temporary home.

"I just put on a pot of coffee," Charlotte said. "It's the hotel's complimentary blend, but it's not bad. Would you like some?"

"Sure. Yes, thank you," Spring answered as Charlotte gestured for her to have a seat on the sofa.

"The boys will be right over," Charlotte said, nodding toward a partially open connecting door.

Spring heard a squeal and then a giggle from the other room. She smiled. The sound of a child's giggle was a good thing.

A moment later, her little patient let out a whoop and ran toward her. She saw a brown body fall on the floor and then a blur of blue launched itself toward her. Spring caught him up with practiced ease.

"My Spring! You came to see me."

She nuzzled his nose. "Of course I did. How are you feeling?"

"Daddy keeps asking me that, too."

"That's because we want to make sure you're all better," she said as she walked to a chair Charlotte had pulled out at the table. "No tummy aches?"

He shook his head.

She sat with him in her lap. "And how's that bandage?"

He lifted up his pajama top so she could see. "Daddy put on a new one. He said he didn't want you to…"

"Hi, Spring," David said from the doorway, where Jeremy had dropped his teddy bear.

Thinking of the conversation with her sisters, Spring smiled. She wondered what bit of information the little boy had been about to blab.

"Hello there," she said as she wrapped her

arms around Jeremy as if to keep him closer for just a bit longer.

"Here you go, Dr. Darling," Charlotte said, placing a plain white mug of steaming coffee on the table, close enough to reach but far away enough to prevent an accidental spill if Jeremy squirmed. "And here's some sugar and creamer."

"Thank you," Spring murmured, her eyes still on David.

What was it about this man that was so compelling? He was for all intents and purposes the enemy when it came to her interests, and she knew she shouldn't be consorting with said enemy. But Spring the woman seemed to have little interest in what Spring the historic conservationist and preservationist wanted. It was a frustrating dichotomy when she let herself think about it.

So she decided that for now she wouldn't think. She would just feel. And this felt right.

She had a sweet little boy in her arms and his gorgeous father was standing there looking like a study in contradictions.

"I got new 'jamas," Jeremy reported, holding out the top of a multicolor Care Bears pajama top. "I got new Pooh, too."

"Did you now? And which one is your favorite?"

"Pooh!"

David approached with Beau, and Jeremy let go of Spring long enough to reach a hand out for his bear.

"Beau ate some banana," the boy reported. The bear just barely missed the coffee, which Spring pushed farther back on the table.

"And did he like it?"

Jeremy nodded. "I had oatmeal with a banana."

Spring glanced up at David. "Good job."

"Jeremy, darling. I think it's time for you to say good-night to Dr. Darling," Charlotte said.

The boy's lower lip trembled as if he might start crying.

Spring pressed a kiss to his head. "My patients have to get a good night's sleep. Doctor's orders."

He nodded, as if hearing the go-to-bed request from Spring carried more weight than the words of his grandmother.

"It was good seeing you again, Jeremy," Spring told him.

"Will you and Daddy tuck us in?"

Spring's heart skipped a beat. She looked at Charlotte for an explanation for the inexplicable request.

"Beau," Charlotte said.

Spring's gaze darted up to David. He unsuccessfully tried to conceal a grin behind his hand.

"If it's all right with your father," Spring finally answered him.

"Of course," David said, pushing off the door frame and heading to the pot of coffee to pour himself a cup.

Jeremy gave Spring the big sloppy kiss that only a four-year-old could bestow. She hugged him close for a moment and then set him on the floor. The boy yawned and placed his hand in his grandmother's.

The two headed back through the open door, and David pulled out the chair opposite of Spring's and took a seat. He doctored his coffee and took a sip.

"Thank you for coming to see him. It means a lot. You've made quite an impression on him."

At a loss for words, Spring nodded and reached for her own cooling cup of joe.

"And on me," he added. "I'm sorry about the way things happened yesterday."

"You were doing your job," she said.

"And you yours. Or at least your other job."

She smiled. "I wear many hats."

"And which one are you wearing now?"

Spring wondered the same thing and thought about her response before answering. "When I called you, I was the preservationist. When I got to the door over there, I was a physician."

"And now?"

She caught her breath.

Was she ready to jump off this cliff? She was

pretty sure there was no net below, just jagged rocks on one side of the crevasse and possibly feathers for a soft landing on the other.

"Would you like to go to dinner with me?" she asked.

"Dinner?"

She flushed. "Well, not dinner for two," she clarified. "I'm in a supper club, the Magnolia Supper Club. We meet once a month to try out new recipes, have some good food and good conversation. It's a small group of what my sister Winter, who is definitely *not* a member, calls 'hoity-toity foodies.' My mother more graciously says the supper club members have discerning palates. We were supposed to meet the other night, but there was a burglary at one of the member's business."

She snapped her mouth shut as if suddenly realizing that she was babbling.

"I'd love to," he said. "When is your next meeting?"

"Tomorrow night," she said. "If that's okay. I know it's short notice. I—"

"What time should I pick you up?"

She smiled. "I can drive."

"I won't hear of it," he said. "If you're supplying dinner, the least I can do is provide the transportation."

"All right," she said. "How about I swing by

here at six and I'll give you the directions. Canapés are at six forty-five. It gives everyone time to arrive and for us to have our business meeting, such as it is. That lasts about five minutes as we pick the next theme."

"What's tomorrow night's theme?"

"It's a surprise," she said.

Charlotte's head poked through the door. "He's all ready for you," she told them.

As Spring and David rose, Spring confided, "I've never tucked anyone in before. Exactly what is involved here?"

"Sometimes a song, sometimes a story." He held his hand out to her. Spring slipped hers into his. "Just follow my lead."

Despite his earlier yawn, Jeremy was sitting on his knees in the middle of the double bed when David and Spring entered the room. Beau was right next to him.

When he saw them, he scrambled under the covers and came back out with a picture book. "This one!"

"Story night," David whispered to Spring. "We've read that one so many times, I think Jeremy can recite it word for word."

The boy got himself and his teddy bear under the light blanket and held the book up for them. Spring watched as David tucked first Beau and then Jeremy in, smoothing the sheet and the blanket over them both.

"Face washed?"

"Check," Jeremy said.

"Teeth brushed?"

"Check."

"Toes tickled?" David said, easily finding the boy's little feet under the covers.

Jeremy giggled and wiggled. "Daaaddy."

David grinned and sat on the edge of the bed. He patted the space beside him for Spring to join him. She did, and a moment later she found herself entranced in the interaction between father and son as David read a short story about a slow train, a fast turtle and a little boy.

By the time he finished, she could see Jeremy was about to nod off. He held on to Beau, though. She heard a little voice say, "Now I lay me down to sleep."

When the prayer was completed, Jeremy turned onto his side, facing them. "I love you, Daddy. I love you, Dr. Spring."

Tears welled in her eyes. She leaned over and kissed him on the forehead. "Good night, Jeremy."

"G'night."

Spring rose, and wiped at her eyes, hoping David hadn't seen her sudden sentimentality.

"I'll be on the other side," she said in a low

voice, then headed toward the relative emotional safety of the next room.

David reached up and turned out the light over Jeremy's bed.

"Daddy?"

He glanced down at Jeremy. "What's up, buddy?"

"I want Dr. Spring to be my mommy."

Chapter Ten

"I'm glad you invited me to join you," David said. "It will be nice to be in the company of adults eating real food."

Spring smiled. "Had your fill of kids' meals and bananas?"

"Just the places that serve them," he answered. "You were right about his appetite and energy returning. When he went flying into your arms last night, it was like nothing had ever happened."

"Children are resilient that way," she said.

He and Spring were en route to the farmhouse for the Magnolia Supper Club's dinner party. A twinge of regret sparked through Spring. She'd invited him to the gathering under false pretenses.

She'd gone to their hotel yesterday to lure him to this dinner. But something had happened to her while in those rooms with David, Jeremy and Charlotte Camden. The invitation she'd extended to him in that moment had been sincere. She really wanted to have dinner with him. But not this way.

Cecelia was right; this wasn't the way to go about getting him to see their point of view on the matter. If anything, it was likely to turn him off, backfiring in her face.

She glanced over at him. "David, I have a confession to make."

He took his eyes off the road for a moment. Long enough to ensure that Spring had his undivided attention. "No confessions or apologies tonight," he said. "Let's just enjoy the evening."

"But…"

He reached for her hand, primly folded in her lap. "No buts," he said. "Tell me more about this supper club of yours. How did it get started, and how did you all come about the name?"

This was safe territory, Spring knew. And in telling him about the club, she could add that members were frequently involved in town events, all the members being longtime residents of Cedar Springs.

"It started as something of an accident," she said, twisting in her seat to face him. "There were a couple of us at a charity event. The dinner was the usual rubber-chicken affair, but the caterer got a little overly creative with the asparagus and the dessert was something that was better off left as individual ingredients in the pantry.

"Gerald Murphy, you'll meet him tonight," she went on, "said something to the effect of 'I wish there was a place I could go to guarantee a decent meal.' Someone else said, 'Well, in that case, stay home and cook it yourself.' And somehow that led to three of us getting together at one of our houses and the subsequent times each of us brought a friend. And then since we were a group, someone suggested a formal arrangement and a name. The rest is cuisine history."

"How about the name?"

"That came from Cecelia. You'll meet her tonight, as well. We were at her place, and she had a lovely centerpiece of magnolia leaves and blossoms. So we became the Magnolia Supper Club. Tonight is a makeup dinner, so to speak," she said.

"Because of the break-in?" he asked. "You mentioned a burglary. What happened?"

She told him about the incident at Step Back in Time Antiques. "Police still have few leads," Spring said. "I'm not sure what had Gerald more upset, the burglary or the cancellation of the dinner."

"Are you…close to this Gerald?"

Something in the tone of his voice, or maybe it was the bit of hesitation she detected, had Spring wondering if maybe he was wondering for personal reasons. So she took care with her answer.

"As close as friends can be. Why?"

He shrugged, and in that movement Spring sensed that there was, indeed, more than idle curiosity on his part.

"When I called you that night, the night Jeremy was sick," he clarified, "you answered the phone thinking I was Gerald."

Spring's brow furrowed. "I did?"

He glanced at her. "You answered and just said, 'Gerald, I'm not giving you a script for Valium.' I figured script was a shortcut for prescription and that you'd need to be pretty close to someone to answer a late-night call with that kind of...specificity."

Spring smiled. "When you meet Gerald, you'll understand. His business partner's wife calls him her special-needs second husband."

"He has a disability?"

"Only if the Americans with Disabilities Act has suddenly started classifying chronic persnicketiness and an overactive use and abuse of hyperbole as a protected disability. Gerald is a lot like the neatnik of *The Odd Couple*, the type where everything must be just so or it makes him crazy. We'd clash like oil and water in any relationship other than friends."

He nodded. "That's good to know," he said quietly and gave her a sidelong glance.

Spring's insides did a little tumble. "Why is that?" she asked, unable to keep the tremble from her voice.

"Lessens the competition," he said.

"Oh."

This time when he glanced her way, there was a smile playing at his mouth, and the butterflies in Spring's stomach took flight. What she couldn't be sure of, though, was the cause of the butterfly swarm. Was it the undeniable attraction she felt toward the man—an attraction that was evident even when she'd thought he was homeless and living in a hotel? Or was it the latent guilt about what she'd set in motion for this evening?

Not too much later, she directed him to the turn off to the farmhouse. Several cars were parked on the grass in front of the house.

"Just pull in wherever you want," Spring said. "It looks like Gerald and Cecelia are here already. Cecelia has a key."

"This is beautiful," David said as he parked.

"Thank you," Spring said. "The house itself dates to the early nineteenth century. You'll see the rooms that are original and the ones that have been added over the years as the family either grew or grew tired of the original footprint, which was small. The ceilings are lower in the original five rooms of the house."

David got out of the car and came around to open Spring's door for her. She murmured her thanks.

"Five rooms," he said. "That was large for the period. We're talking the early 1800s, right?"

She nodded as she slipped her hand into his. "Yes, 1825. There was a kitchen and a front room and three bedrooms. A double outhouse was over there," she said, pointing to an area near a copse of cedar trees. "They were highfalutin," she added with a laugh. "Wealthy for the time. The Darlings always had a lot of children. In the case of the great-great-grandparents who built the place, there were the two of them, their seven kids and eventually all of their many children and grandchildren. That's one of the reasons my mother is so frantic about us producing grandchildren. She has a huge house like all of the Darlings for generations and not one of us has presented her with a baby to spoil."

"Was marriage and kids not something you wanted?"

"It's not that I don't want a family," Spring said. "I always thought by this age I'd have kids in middle school, that I'd be shuttling little ones to soccer and ballet and piano lessons."

She stopped talking, and David stopped walking. They were at the base of a large oak tree; its branches provided shade for the side of the house.

"What happened?" he asked, lifting his free hand to tame hair that had escaped her updo.

"It didn't work out that way," Spring said with what she hoped came off as a nonchalant shrug. "Anyway, I did end up with a lot of kids," she continued, aiming to put a bright face on the matter. "I'm a pediatrician. I look at all of my young patients as my children. I have their well-being at heart as much as, and sometimes more than, their parents."

He was quiet for a moment, then said, "I see what you mean. But it's not the same thing. Kids change your focus. Instead of I and me, your focus shifts to what's most important for this little person who is depending on you for everything. You pray and hope you don't mess it up, that maybe you learned something from the way you were raised, something that will make it all work out for the best."

"Jeremy is a good boy," Spring said.

"He calls you pretty Spring."

She smiled. "I know. I don't know why he calls me that, but every time he says it, it's just the sweetest thing."

"When he was sick, you made him better.

When he opened his eyes, he saw what I see when I look at you."

Spring's gaze lifted to meet his. "What's that?"

Her question was just barely a whisper. They were so close she breathed in the musky citrus of his aftershave or cologne and liked the scent that seemed so much a part of him.

"A woman of infinite beauty and grace."

"David."

Saying his name was like releasing a cavalcade of emotions she didn't even realize was locked up inside her.

"Spring, I'm going to kiss you now."

"I know," she said.

And then his mouth covered hers in an embrace that left her breathless.

Spring wondered at the way her heart beat seemingly in unison with his. Every fiber of her seemed to be saying that this was right, this was what it felt like to love and to be loved.

But her head was sending another message, one that she let drown out the drumbeat of her heart. She pulled away and stared up at him.

"Do you want me to apologize?" he asked.

Unable to speak, Spring just shook her head from side to side.

"I…" She paused, then lifted a finger to his mouth to trace its contours.

David caught her hand, opened her palm and pressed a kiss into it.

"Let's go inside," he said. "Dinner and your friends are waiting."

That had the effect of a glass of ice water in the face. Spring stepped back, putting needed distance between them and claiming her hand from him.

"David, this is more than just a dinner party."

He grinned. "I know."

Her eyes widened. "You do? But how? Who told you?"

"You did," he said.

Spring was 250 percent sure that she had done no such thing. She hadn't mentioned it to anyone but the supper club members since she'd concocted this harebrained intervention dinner party. "When?"

"When you told me you wanted me to meet some of your friends," he said, reaching for and tugging on her hand. "Come on—let's not keep them waiting."

"That's not what I meant," she said.

But he either didn't hear or chose to ignore her protestation.

While the Magnolia Supper Club's dinner commenced at the Darling family's historic farmhouse, another burglary was under way in downtown Cedar Springs.

It was a quick affair, the items to steal pretargeted and the business's less than stellar alarm easy for the two-person burglary crew to overcome. In and out they went. They tucked their goods in the trunk of a dark sedan, a four-door vehicle that looked like many, many others in the city. And then they were off, headed out to Orchard Road where merchandise was stored, repackaged and prepared for delivery to willing buyers.

The diners were seated following introductions over hors d'oeuvres. Among the supper club members were Roger and Carol Delaney, who owned a bed-and-breakfast; Maddie Powers, who was a retired home economics teacher; and Natalie and Christopher Parker, who were self-proclaimed foodies and hosted an online food podcast. As host of the meal, Gerald explained to his guests what he'd prepared.

"The lovely Cecelia has offered to assist me, and thank you to Spring for opening your home for our little soiree."

After the group decided on the next gathering's theme and host, Gerald provided descriptions of the meal he'd prepared. "We'll begin with a fennel and apple salad with lemon shallot, followed by a fresh corn chowder with feta and sun-dried tomatoes. Then," he said, practically beaming with glee and pride, "we shall feast on trout stuffed with salmon mousse in a deliriously light puff pastry along with a yummy yam soufflé."

"Sounds scrumptious."

"It is," Gerald said. "And that's not boasting," he added to chuckles from his supper club members. "For dessert, well, I'll tell you about that later, but you are absolutely going to die of bliss."

The courses and conversation flowed around the table, touching on everything from alternative ways to prepare the entrée to an update on the burglary at Step Back in Time Antiques.

"Do the police have any leads?"

"If you mean like something that will lead them to whomever burglarized the store, no," Gerald said with a huff. "But I have some leads of my own."

"I'm afraid to ask," Maddie Powers said.

"You don't have to," Gerald said. "I'm going to tell you."

"That's what I was afraid of," Carol Delaney said, reaching for her water goblet.

Spring and David shared a glance, humor sparking between them. "I told you," Spring murmured. "Maddie has had a thing for him for years. He's oblivious."

"Hey, no whispering down there," Cecelia

said. "If you're sharing juicy gossip, I want to be a part of it."

"Just filling him in on some backstory," Spring said.

David lifted his water goblet in a slight toast to indicate all was well at their end of the table.

"On the QT, Officer Walters told me that the police are looking into several burglaries in Cedar Springs," Gerald said, clearly relishing his role as purveyor of news unknown to the others. "And," he said, lowering his voice as if said criminals might be listening in to their dinner conversation, "they think there may be a ring operating somewhere out here."

"Out here where?" Cecelia asked.

"In one of the abandoned barns or houses," Gerald said. "Can you imagine that?"

Spring's eyes widened, and she looked at Cecelia, who was also staring at Gerald.

"There aren't that many abandoned properties," Spring said. "Many of them are like this house, used as weekend getaways."

Gerald nodded knowingly. "Exactly. I would assume the crooks have scanned out all of the property out here and know exactly when they're empty. They could be watching us right now."

"Gerald," Cecelia said, "stop being so melodramatic."

He huffed and sat back. "Call it what you

want. I just hope the police recover those paintings and the vases they took. I can't believe they just cherry-picked our inventory like that."

Cecelia pushed her chair back. "I'm going to go get dessert ready," she said, standing. "Spring, why don't you help me?"

Spring knew exactly what Cecelia wanted to talk to her about in the privacy of the kitchen. They'd seen Sweet Willie wandering around in the area where there was a barn that was definitely deserted. What if he was a part of the burglary ring or knew something about it?

Just as soon as they were alone in the big country kitchen, Cecelia voiced the very question that had been on Spring's mind.

"Do you think Sweet Willie has something to do with the break-in at the antiques store?"

Spring leaned against the counter. "I don't know. It doesn't seem likely."

"What's out here for a homeless man to get into besides trouble?" Cecelia said, keeping her voice low so it didn't carry to the other room. "Wasn't I just saying yesterday something was off about him?"

"Do you think we should go to the police?" Spring said.

"Go to the police about what?" David asked, entering the kitchen with several dinner plates in hand.

Spring started as if she herself had been caught in the middle of a criminal activity. She looked at Cecelia, who lifted and dropped her shoulders, leaving the decision to Spring whether or not to bring David into their confidence. Although he was an outsider, she trusted him… Well, she trusted certain parts of him. But because he wasn't from Cedar Springs, maybe he could see a different perspective.

"Cecelia and I were coming out here to get the house ready for this dinner, putting the leaves in the table, making sure there was enough dinnerware and that sort of thing. But on the way here, we saw one of the homeless men who is a regular for meals at Manna, the Common Ground ministry's soup kitchen."

"Was he doing something illegal?" David asked.

"No," Spring said.

"But there's a good reason to believe he's not so innocent."

"Cecelia," Spring said, resignation in her voice.

"What?" David asked, looking between the two women.

"Cecelia has a theory about him that I think is ridiculous."

David placed the dirty dishes in the sink. "Well, if there's a connection between him and the burglary at Gerald's store, you should let the authorities know. Police on the news are always saying that even the smallest of details can be significant to a case."

"What do you think, CeCe?"

The professor looked torn as she weighed the pros and cons of the situation.

"Tell you what," Cecelia finally said, "I have some volunteer shifts at Manna this coming week. If Sweet Willie is there, I'll see what he has to say."

"You should not be playing detective," Spring said. "We have no idea what, if anything, could be going on."

"That's right," David said. "I've been involved with development projects where squatters had to be forcibly removed from buildings before demolition or renovation could take place. It wasn't pretty, and the police were ultimately called in on each situation. Given that you're thinking there could be criminal activity associated, the wisest course of action would be alerting the authorities."

Spring let out a snort, the type her mother would deem extremely unladylike. She went to the refrigerator and started pulling out the miniature parfaits that would be served with their tortoni.

"If you think Professor Many Degrees over

there is going to follow the wisest course of any action, you'll be sadly and extremely mistaken."

"Professor Many Degrees?"

"Pay her no attention whatsoever," Cecelia answered.

But Spring was looking at David. "What you said," she told him. "That may be it."

"What did I say?"

"The abandoned buildings. My sister Summer runs the kitchen at Manna. And I remember her saying there have been periods when Sweet Willie just sort of disappeared."

"And?" Cecelia prompted.

"The abandoned buildings out here. They are the perfect place for someone to live, especially someone without a permanent home," she said. "Maybe that's what Sweet Willie was doing out on Orchard Road. Heading to a barn or building where he's—what did you call it?—squatting?"

David nodded. "It's not as big a problem here on the East Coast as it is in some of the southwestern and western states where entire subdivisions have foreclosed properties. Homeless people, drug addicts and others just move in. Sometimes squatters keep up a property better than the homeowners who abandoned the places because they want it to appear like they belong there."

"How long does it take three adults to gather

a simple dessert?" Gerald said, entering the kitchen carrying the remaining dinner dishes. With a glance around the kitchen, he scowled. "You didn't put the coffee on. Must I do everything?"

"No one makes chicory coffee like you do, Gerald," Spring said, smoothly changing the subject.

"Go," Gerald said, shooing all three out of the room. "I'll see to the dessert and coffee service."

After dessert at the dining room table, the group of diners moved to the living room for after-dinner coffee and the real purpose of the dinner party.

"So, David," Carol Delaney said. "I read in the *Gazette* that your firm is coming up with a plan for developing outlying parcels here in Cedar Springs."

"That's right," he said, taking a sip of espresso from the demitasse cup. "My team has reviewed all of the sites, but I've only seen two of the three proposed sites. I'm here to inspect the third."

Cecelia, sitting to his left, reached for one of the small fresh-baked minibiscottis on a tray that Spring was passing around. "Did you know that this house was once part of the Underground Railroad? One of Spring's ancestors was an abolitionist."

"Really?" David said, sitting forward. "I

researched a lot of the area and didn't come across that fact. I know there were rumors about way stations being in eastern North Carolina, but I had no idea that Cedar Springs was a part of it."

Cecelia nodded and continued with the story. "Cedar Springs was something of a little protected enclave in the years leading to the War. Things weren't quite as they appeared. Most of the homes over on Catalpa Road, like the Scofield House, are on the Historic Register. They were all built by and for free blacks."

"Cecelia heads up a project that's getting a few of the ones that haven't been kept up purchased and renovated."

"Is that so?" David said. "Hmm…"

Spring wondered what he was thinking. But before she could think of a way to ask, Cecelia was answering.

"Indeed," the professor said. "There were more free blacks living in the town, then known as Springs, North Carolina, than in much of the state. Spring's family, the Darlings, were a perfect example of how it was done. A couple believed by most to be their enslaved domestics were actually a teacher and a groomsman who would later go on to earn a medical degree. Eventually that groom earned the piece of paper that validated what he'd been doing most of his life under the tutelage of Dr. Darling, her great-great-grandfather," she said with a nod toward Spring.

"And that black teacher who masqueraded as a house servant for the Darling family was her grandmother's grandmother," Spring said, indicating Cecelia.

"Hiding in plain sight," David said. Then he sat back in the wing chair and steepled his hands. "I'm starting to get the overall picture here," he added. "You didn't invite me here for dinner. This is some sort of passive-aggressive ploy to get me to either withdraw from the mixed-use project or to recommend one of the other sites."

He didn't look at Spring when he made the accusation, but she felt his quiet wrath as if he were yelling directly at her.

Sitting forward, David met the anxious gazes of each of the dinner party guests. "I don't appreciate the subterfuge," he said. "If you wanted to make your case, why couldn't you be straight up about it?"

For an uncomfortable moment, the room remained oddly quiet. *The quiet of the guilty*, Spring thought.

"Don't blame them," she said, looking as miserable as she felt. She'd been trying to tell him, to make her confession before things got to this point. But she had waited too late, let herself get swept up in the tide of *it'll all work out in the end.* She should have known better. Only in the movies and on reality television did interventions actually end with the result desired at the beginning. "It was my idea," she told David. "As a matter of fact, more than one person tried to talk me out of it. I just thought—"

"You just thought that you could bombard me with stories about how precious this house and your land is. How I should take my architectural plans and go ruin some other community."

Spring lowered her head.

That's exactly what she'd thought. But hearing the words come from David made the plan seem cold and callous, devious and self-serving.

"We thought if you saw—"

David held up a hand to halt the rest of her explanation. Rising, he nodded to the members of the Magnolia Supper Club. "The food was great," he said. "I wish I could say the same about the rest of the evening." When no one said anything, he added, "I'll see myself out."

Spring slumped in her seat.

She would have liked to have heard the front door slam behind him on his way out. But there wasn't even that bit of his anger to assuage her guilt.

"I'm sorry, guys," she told her friends. "This clearly wasn't one of my better ideas."

"What do we do now?" Carol asked.

"Maybe we can fast-track the historic landmark application."

Spring rose. "Excuse me," she told her friends. "I need some air."

She didn't want to cry, but she felt the wetness welling up in her eyes. Cecelia had predicted that this escapade would end badly. Spring had relied on the strength of her convictions. But look where that got her—roundly and solidly chastised by someone she was starting to have strong feelings for.

Pulling open the front door, she came up short when she spied David standing on the porch. His back was to her as he stood gazing out at the cedar trees and beyond them the fields leased by small farming operations.

"I thought you'd left."

"I wanted to," he said without turning around. "But I hoped you would come out."

Still standing in the doorway, the screen door open, Spring asked, "Why?"

"Because even more than I wanted to leave, I wanted to hear from you why you did this. Why you thought it would be all right to lure me under false pretenses out here to your family's home. Was it so you and your friends could have some fun at my expense?"

Chapter Eleven

"That wasn't the case at all," she said, dismayed by the very idea.

Spring closed the door and indicated the swing on the front porch. "Would you like to sit?" she asked.

"No."

He had yet to face her. He stood on the top step, hands shoved in his pockets, his back erect. Spring imagined he was holding on to his temper with everything he had in him. She knew if the tables were reversed, she'd be giving him more than a piece of her mind; she would be giving him the riot act with a righteous dose of Southern indignation.

Spring moved forward until she stood next to him.

"I'm sorry," she said as she, too, stared into the distance. "It seemed like a good way to introduce you to some of the members of the historical society. What you saw at the planning commission meeting was, well, a more vocal faction, and things got out of hand."

"At least Mrs. Lundsford was honest and upfront about where she stood."

"I was angry," she said. "When you walked into that room and I realized who you were and what your business was here, I was just…" She shook her head. "Ambushing you seemed irresistible. Gerald, Cecelia and I along with Roger and Carol Delaney and Johnson Gray are all historical society members as well as in the supper club. We…" She paused. "No, *I* thought we could show rather than tell you how much this property means not just to me and my family but to the history of Cedar Springs. Don't blame them for a plan that was my idea."

She chanced a glance in his direction to see how her words affected him.

If they had any type of impact, it didn't show. She could read nothing in the features, which had grown hard right before her eyes.

"You made me the butt of the joke with your friends."

"It wasn't intended that way," Spring said, feeling miserable about what she had done. "I won't harbor you any ill will if your recommendation is for land the Darlings own, either outright or in trust."

He snorted. "In trust? You mean you own even more of the town?"

Spring's eyes narrowed. "Every bit of real estate that my family owns is in the public record."

"I'm sure it is," he said drily.

Spring's pique at him was starting to take wing. "David, staging an intervention of sorts wasn't one of my better ideas, but it was well intended," she said, gathering steam for her argument. "There are a lot of people in Cedar Springs, in eastern North Carolina, who could care less about the history of this place. But there are a lot who do. We can't just have placards or road markers put up at every site that has historic significance. All of the state would be one big 'This happened here in 1789 or 1882 or 1952 or yesterday' sign. But we can keep that history alive, the history of then and the history we're making now."

She went down a couple of steps and spread her hand out to indicate the acres of land surrounding the house. "Green space is to be cherished," she said. "It may look like a lot to you, someone who makes a living getting maximum density out of every available square foot of land, but there are only so many shopping centers and subdivisions and mixed-use developments that a city or town needs.

"You and Mayor Howell are expecting some sort of population boom. You're operating under the pie-in-the-sky notion of if you build it, they will come."

She came up one step so that she stood just beneath him. "The earth," she said, "this ground, is all there is. We can't grow another."

He folded his arms across his chest. "Spring, tell me something. What did you hope to get out of this—dinner party—today?" he said putting an emphasis on dinner party, letting her know he knew it was anything but a party.

"I wanted you to see how much of Cedar Springs is actually living history."

"So all of that business about your and Cecelia's great-great-grandparents was just fabrication to make the story more compelling?"

She shook her head. "It's all true," she said. "Cecelia is one of the preeminent African American historians here in North Carolina. She's a Rhodes Scholar, has degrees from Duke, Harvard and Oxford. All of them doctorates. She can trace her ancestry almost as far back as I can. We both believe in historic preservation," she added, putting emphasis on the word *preservation*, "not just footnotes in history books. If we don't preserve the past, it will be forgotten."

David let out a puff of air, then relaxed his arms.

"Where the city council ultimately decides to put a mixed-used development isn't up to me."

"No, but just like with what happened with the planning commission, you'll make a recommendation and that recommendation will hold sway with the council."

His mouth quirked up in what could only be described as a sardonic smile. "So your Not-In-My-Backyard campaign is about getting this in another part of town?"

Summer shook her head. "It's not about this parcel of land or the ones you call parcels one and three. If we had our druthers, there would be little or no new development in the city. There's plenty here to preserve or to restore. But we, the historical society members, recognize that time marches on, names are forgotten. And in this case, if a road is built through here, the final resting places of countless men and women and children will be right here, under tons of concrete and asphalt, lost forever until a millennia from now explorers and archaeologists come through wondering what it all means. We have the opportunity here and now to give our children's children something to be proud of."

"You make a strong case," David said. "But you've forgotten one crucial fact."

"What's that?" she asked, her nose screwed up in irritation.

"It's not my call to make. The city council votes on where they want the development. My role is to create uses for space, to make land-use recommendations."

"That's just it," Spring said. "Don't you see? What you design will be here for a long, long time. The homes and businesses built to your plans can enhance or detract from Cedar Springs. I'm not naive, David. And I'm not antidevelopment. What I am concerned about is how and if the city will mark and honor this new phase of its growth. With respect to what you do, your new urbanism plan, homes with shops and businesses to walk to and whatnot, is more of the same and misses the mark."

"And having a sit-down adult business meeting doesn't fit in with that concern?"

Spring, remembering the kiss they'd shared just a couple of hours ago, tried to reconcile that strong and appealing man with the cold and calculating businessman in front of her now.

No, she thought. Not cold and calculating— he was cold and ambivalent. And given the way she'd gone about this dinner party, maybe he had a right to be.

What Cedar Springs needed was not historical society members waving their banners about what happened twenty-five, fifty, one hundred or two hundred years ago. What they needed was a public relations initiative—to get the message out there.

Even as she looked at David Camden watching her, Spring's mind was jumping forward, considering and then discarding the local firms that flashed through her mental Rolodex file of contacts and acquaintances. They didn't need a lawyer to file lawsuits, they needed an image consultant, someone who could generate support and reshape public opinion by showing the benefits of preservation. Then she hit on a name: Trey Calloway at Keaton & Myers, a top-tier management consulting firm that had offices in town. The Calloway family's history in Cedar Springs ran deep, about as deep as Spring's and Cecelia's. Trey Calloway would be able to understand and appreciate the delicate task of balancing preservation and progress.

In the meantime, she could share what she loved with David Camden…if he'd let her.

Spring held out her hand in both invitation and supplication. "David, I'd like to show you some things."

"What? Do you have more historical society

members in the barn with digestifs to finish the Magnolia Supper Club's little soiree?"

"No," she said. "It's just us. I want to show you the farm."

"Farm?"

She nodded and waited for him to make up his mind about joining her.

After what seemed an interminable period, he nodded and took a step down, clasping her hand in his. They walked a short distance from the house.

"My earliest memory is of this house and lands, of feeding ducks at this pond," she told him. "I had to have been three or maybe almost four. Winter was an infant, I remember that because I was upset that a crying, pooping, squiggly pink thing had usurped my position in the house. Mom and Dad didn't seem to notice me anymore. In my young opinion, they were only interested in the baby. We were living here then. Daddy had not yet built The Compound for Mom or the space that would be his office."

"What was a four-year-old doing alone near a pond?"

"Exactly my grandmother's question," Spring said. "She must have seen me leave the house and followed me. There was a family of ducks, a mama and her ducklings, who would come here to sun themselves."

Spring took off her shoes and stood at the water's edge as if the ducks from long ago were still there waiting for her.

"Without scolding me for venturing away from the house, Grandma put some bread crumbs in my hand and told me to toss them out for the ducks. The mama duck, she explained, had a lot of work to do. She needed to tend to the babies while looking out for predators like hawks, who would swoop down and snatch a baby, or the hounds that liked to chase the ducks until they tired, leaving them too exhausted to fend off other hungry predators."

"So she likened your parents with the new baby to the mother duck?"

"Exactly," Spring said. "The lesson I learned that day, the one that stayed with me for the rest of my life, was that the elders have to care for and look out for the younger ones, be they human or animal. You know, the least of us."

David nodded. "I see the parallel to the Scripture in Matthew."

"So," Spring said, "I stopped resenting my little sister. It's a good thing I did since two more would come in short order. I took the whole older sister bit to heart. Probably too much, they would say," she added. "But the die was cast. Later, as I grew up and could appreciate it more, my grandfather told me about the history of this land, the slaves who came through on their way to freedom. The migrants who worked the fields here before heading north to the eastern shores of both Virginia and Maryland.

"I soaked all of that information in, David. I became a living and breathing history lesson."

"What does that have to do with the mixed-use development project?"

"Everything," she said. "I became a doctor because that's in my DNA. My father and my grandfather were doctors. But from my grandmothers, I got the love of and appreciation for history. I don't want this land preserved because I want it in my family. I want it preserved so all of the families in Cedar Springs and elsewhere can learn the stories of what this area meant."

"Then why haven't you done something about it?" David asked. "All I see is a nice house, some well-maintained fields and nothing else."

Spring was hoping he'd ask.

"Cecelia and I are in the process of writing a grant application for just that," she said, hoping the note of pride and confidence she heard in her own voice didn't sound quite as sanctimonious as she thought it did. "Until Mayor Howell popped up with this mixed-use development idea, there was no need to announce or make public what we were working on. All the pieces were fitting together. My family was donating the land to the project. We had a solid business plan. All we needed was the rest of the funding."

She looked away for a moment and sighed heavily. "We learned the hard way about making things public before all the i's were dotted and all the t's crossed."

"What do you mean?"

She then told him the history of the Junction at Commerce Plaza. "The historical society wanted that land to build a history and interpretive center. Before we knew it, though, gas pumps and twenty-four-hour flashing lights were there. That junction—we believed then and still believe now—has a major historical site beneath it, a mill and a cemetery. But because the project was rushed through and done so hush-hush without anything approximating public comment, we'll never know for sure now."

"Hmm," he said. "So, this history and interpretive center you're talking about would be here?"

Spring nodded. "With an archeological research aspect to it. That's where the grant writing comes in," she said. "When we say 'history' or 'archeology' to the public, people's eyes generally glaze over. But that doesn't have to be the case. There are actually waiting lists for the seminars Cecelia teaches at the university."

"Why didn't you just tell me this?" David asked. "Why lure me into the lion's den to attack?"

She sighed again. "This is going to sound lame, and it is lame, but, well, it seemed like it a good idea at the time. It was the best I could come up with. Things seem to be moving very fast as far as the city's official channels are concerned."

He contemplated her for a moment, as if weighing the veracity of her words. She tried to imagine how she would feel if their roles and the situation were reversed.

"That's not good enough, Spring," he said.

"I thought you might say something like that."

She leaned her head back and regarded the sky for a moment as if the right words might shower down on her. When she faced him again, it was with a newfound resolve.

"There's a bench over there," she said, indicating a shady grove a few yards away. She didn't wait for him to respond to the implied invitation; she just starting walking toward it, her shoe straps dangling in her hands.

She had to make this man, this man she was starting to care way too much about despite their differences, she had to make him understand why this meant so much to her.

They settled on the wooden bench, placed

strategically by one of her grandparents for optimum views of both the pond and the garden.

He indicated with a motion of his head that he was ready to listen to her.

Spring wasn't quite sure where to begin and told him just that.

"Then start at the beginning," he said.

Her laugh sounded to her ears more bitter than humor filled. "That, my friend, would take all night."

"I don't mind."

The softly spoken words startled her, and she tucked a foot under herself as she faced him. For a moment, she said nothing, just stared into eyes that held no censure. What she saw was patience and promise and something else she recognized: gentleness and understanding. Maybe David Camden, and what his company represented, was not the enemy as she'd initially perceived him at the planning commission meeting. Maybe he was simply a man who believed in what he did as strongly as she believed in the causes and programs that were her own personal passions.

And maybe the beginning is where she needed to start.

"My sisters and I," she began, "grew up in a wealthy family. But we were all taught from a very young age that to whom much is given, much is required. Summer, Winter, Autumn and I learned by the examples set for us by our parents and grandparents. Giving to the community in some form or fashion wasn't just expected—it was simply part of having the Darling last name."

When he nodded, she continued. "My father and grandfather were doctors who worked long hours, and their wives, my mother and grandmother, were far from simply the garden club ladies who lunched. Granted, Lovie does both and in style, but she also gets her hands dirty." She smiled. "You're probably wondering what this has to do with anything."

He reached for her hand and laced his fingers with hers. "The thought had crossed my mind."

Her mouth quirked up in amusement at that as she contemplated their joined hands.

"How old were you when you had Jeremy?"

"Is that your roundabout way of asking how old I am? I'm thirty-six. Jeremy is four."

"I'm thirty-five," she said. "When I was a little girl, there was no doubt that I would be a doctor. That's all I ever wanted to do. But I also assumed I'd have a family, a husband and children to share my life. When I started college, I knew that by thirty-two—the age you were when Jeremy was born—I just knew for sure that I would be living the white-picket-fence life. Preferably here at the farmhouse because of course the man I married would want to live here," she added with a small, wry laugh. "But it didn't happen that way for me. And so when I finished medical school, I gave all of my energy to the work that I loved. That meant building not just my career, but my community. Before long, that's all there was. It's who I am and what I am."

"You're wrong, Spring," he said, the words so quiet she would have missed them had she not been sitting right next to him. "You're more than how you fill the hours of each day."

"I know," she said. "I have my family, my sisters and mother, good friends, an active church community—"

He paused the rush of words with a finger at her mouth.

"Do you know why I was first attracted to you?"

Her eyes darted across his features, indicating the confusion his words wrought.

He chuckled. "Now you're wondering if I've changed the subject."

She tugged a bit in order to release his hand from hers, but he held on tighter, forcing her to remain seated beside him on the bench even though his intensity made her want to flee.

A moment later he released her hand. Spring didn't move from her spot on the seat.

He continued talking as if the little tug-of-war hadn't happened. "You were beautiful and the MD on your lab coat assured me that you would see to my son's health and well-being. But I saw something else in you," David told her. "I saw an innate goodness. That's something that can't be playacted. It's either there or it isn't. And I saw it in abundance in you."

"David…"

"Let me finish," he said, taking her hand again, this time letting her palm rest in his. "We clearly don't see eye to eye on this project. But I'd like to believe I have an open mind. Tell me something, Spring. Was this so-called Magnolia Supper Club intervention the only reason you invited me to dinner?"

"That's what I was trying to tell you in the car as we drove out here. I…" She paused for a moment, got her thoughts together. This was the crux of it in one simple question. She knew that a lot was riding on her answer. He wasn't just talking about a municipal development versus historic preservation. The question was personal, and she knew it. It was about them, just the two of them. Spring and David as individuals. As a couple.

A couple?

A part of her wanted to hedge. It could all go horribly wrong. And probably would. But she wanted to take the chance. Wasn't life about taking chances, the road less traveled and all of that? It had taken years to mend her heart after it had been broken the last time. Until David Camden and that sweetheart of a son of his had walked into the Common Ground Free Clinic, she hadn't noticed a man, not dared to expose her heart to the possibility of love. But now? Now she was willing to take that chance, make that leap.

"No. It's not the only reason I invited you," she answered him, taking the jump and hoping a net or some feathers or something soft would break her fall.

Chapter Twelve

That conversation marked a turning point for them. When they returned to the house, it was to find anxious faces waiting for them.

"We decided to be adult about this," David said.

Gerald slumped with relief into the wing-back chair where he'd been perched with a demitasse cup. "Oh, thank goodness. We were beginning to wonder if one of you had murdered the other out there."

"Nothing so dramatic," Spring said. "Did you save any biscotti?"

With the air clear in the room and another tray of biscotti passed around, David asked for more information about the history of Cedar Springs.

It was close to midnight when they finally arrived back in the parking lot at David's hotel. He walked her to her car.

"Thank you for an…interesting evening," he said.

"I'm sorry. Really sorry."

"Water under the bridge," he assured her. "After the drama, I actually learned quite a bit. Information that I didn't know, wouldn't have guessed and that my team back in Charlotte hadn't discovered."

Spring groaned, and her shoulders slumped. "I've made things worse for us. I suppose this is a just punishment for being dishonest with you. You're going full speed ahead with your plans to—"

He halted her words with a finger on her lips again, and a heartbeat later his finger was replaced by his mouth on hers.

The kiss was so light and sweet that Spring responded before realizing just what she was doing—kissing him back.

He released her and took a step back. "My plans haven't changed, Spring. And neither have yours. What's changed between us is that we're each a little more willing to see the other's perspective on the matter."

"That's true," she said, wondering at the almost breathless voice she barely recognized as her own.

"Since you insist on apologizing, how about a proper one?"

She eyed him with sudden suspicion. "What exactly do you mean?"

"A date," he said. "A real one. Just the two of us. With no talk of my work or yours the entire time."

She grinned and held her hand out. He clasped it in his.

"Deal," she said.

That Saturday they both conceded that who they were and what they were would probably seep into their conversation at some point, but they would use any such moment to discuss their differences rationally.

It was a great plan and would have worked had they not stopped by Step Back in Time Antiques. She'd mentioned the antique train set that was on display at the store and how it had reminded her of Jeremy that very first night. Then to discover one of his favorite books was about a train—they had to stop and see it, she said.

Gerald Murphy saw them and waved them in with a frantic wave.

"Spring, David. You aren't going to believe what's happened," he wailed.

Alarmed, Spring grabbed her friend's arm. "What's happened?"

"A burglary!" he said, ushering them deeper into the store.

"No," Spring exclaimed. "Not again. What was taken?"

"Not here," Gerald said. "Down the street at Object d'Art. It happened the night of our dinner. This is horrible, just horrible. What's happened to our lovely little city?"

Richard came out of the office with a plump woman in her midfifties behind him and assessed the situation. He tucked his reading glasses on top of his head. "Well, I see Gerald has shared the disturbing news."

"Hi, Annette," Spring said. She quickly introduced David to both Richard and his wife, then asked, "What happened?"

"It was horrible!" Gerald said. "I think I need something to calm my nerves."

"Try some tea," Spring intoned drily. "Tea Time down the street has a specialty blend that's just what the doctor ordered."

Gerald huffed and turned back toward the office, leaving his business partner to fill in the details of the city's crime spree.

Richard shook his head. "He needs a vacation."

"He needs a wife," Annette said.

"What woman would have him? She'd have to

be a neurotic hypochondriac like him or they'd make each other crazy."

"Maddie Powers is perfect for him," Annette said.

Spring all but stamped her foot. "Richard, what happened at the art gallery?"

The antiques dealer sighed. "The same sort of thing that happened to us," he said. "The police said a person or persons unknown broke in about nine o'clock. Walked in, selected three pieces— one of them on loan from the Tate's modern art collection. Poor Allison," he said. "She had to call Miranda and tell her what happened."

Spring filled in the blanks for David. "Allison is the gallery's assistant manager. She's been holding down the fort, so to speak, while the owner has been recuperating from an illness. And the Tate is a British—"

"I'm familiar with its museums and galleries."

"What in the world is going on around here?"

Annette hustled to the Hepplewhite writing desk that served as the store's checkout area. David's gaze followed her, and his eyes widened. He stood gaping at the piece of furniture.

"Reproduction, right?"

Annette laughed. "Hardly. Thank goodness our burglars didn't have your eye."

"Is it…?"

"Not for sale," Richard said, coming up behind

him with Spring. "And with these crimes suddenly plaguing downtown, we may move it to the house."

"Here it is," Annette said as she handed a flier to Spring. "The police came by with this. Chief Llewelyn has called an open meeting for merchants and residents to provide information about the incidents."

Spring read the flier and handed it to David, who read it without comment.

"Are you going?" Spring asked.

"Of course. We were the first victims, and we hope poor Allison and Miranda were the last."

When Spring and David returned to her car, Spring sat at the wheel in silence for a bit.

"What are you thinking?"

"Thoughts that I'd rather not," she said. "I was thinking about something Cecelia and I saw the other day." She relayed the information about Sweet Willie out on Orchard Road.

"You think he's a thief?"

Spring shook her head. "No. But these burglaries and what we were talking about at the supper club, about the squatters, it seems…" She shrugged. "I don't know. Not necessarily connected. But related. I want to check on something out at the farm if you don't mind."

"The farm?"

"The farmhouse, or rather the land and buildings around it," she clarified.

Spring leaned over and looked at his feet. "What kind of shoes are you wearing?"

"Loafers, why?"

She frowned. "Those won't do." She peered closer at his legs and feet.

"Spring?"

"I think Dad's waders will fit you."

"Waders? Where are we going?"

She straightened and started the car. "To check a hunch."

More than two hours later, that hunch paid off. She'd parked her car at the farmhouse and swapped it for a battered but excellently running pickup truck that she backed out of the garage. Her father's old hip waders did fit David, who was still asking exactly what they were doing.

"A land survey," Spring said. "Right up your alley."

From the house she retrieved a rolled-up map that she tossed on the dash of the pickup.

"We're going to do something that we—my sisters and I—should have been doing for some time. Inspecting the outbuildings on Darling land. We have someone who comes to tend to the house and the land immediately around it, but, as you know, most of this is undeveloped and there are plenty of seemingly abandoned buildings."

"How much land are we talking about?"

She glanced at him. "About five hundred acres."

They found what they were looking for not in the outermost buildings, but tucked in the easily overlooked middle section of the property.

"You know," David said, "I kept looking at this area on the Google Earth image. The elevation seemed unnaturally high for this topography."

Spring sighed as they looked at the old building. "This area isn't a true switchback. But as you saw, the road isn't a road and has curves, just close enough that everyone knows what we mean."

"When were you last here?"

"Never," Spring said. "That's why I brought the map that has all of the outbuildings marked. We need to call the police. Something tells me they're going to be really interested in this."

The building, which had the look of an old bunkhouse for field laborers, was chockablock full of large boxes that very clearly had not been sitting empty for the past thirty or so years. The electronic equipment they discovered in one was further proof that the space was being used as some sort of illicit, and very modern, storage facility.

While they waited for the police to arrive, Spring called her mother, her sisters, the family's lawyer and a Durham-based security firm.

The responding officers alerted the police chief, who personally came out to the scene. Several hours later, after answering questions from both Chief Llewelyn and his investigating officer, and then with those officers inspecting all the other outbuildings on the family's land, the five Darling women, Cameron Jackson and David Camden gathered at the farmhouse. In the country kitchen, Summer sliced apples for pies, Autumn Darling paced the room and Lovie Darling sat at the table asking the same question they'd been asking each other and the police for several hours.

"How could this have happened? A burglary ring using my property as a warehouse."

"Easily enough," Cameron said, filching an apple slice from his fiancée's bowl of sliced apples. She slapped his hand away, but he grinned and planted a kiss on her cheek. "No one is out here on any sort of regular basis."

"Well, that's clearly changing as of immediately," Autumn said. "I'll move my stuff out here in the morning."

"Out of the question," Lovie said. "Those criminals are sure to be back looking for their stuff."

"By this time, I'm sure they know it's been confiscated," Spring said. "And I've already contracted with a firm for twenty-four-hour patrols until we can decide what to do on a more permanent basis."

Lovie glanced at Summer, who was adding cinnamon, sugar and lemon juice to the bowl. "Sweetheart, I think you've baked enough pies for one evening."

Summer looked at the counter, where five apple pies were cooling. "Nervous energy," she said. "I'll take them to Manna tomorrow."

Cameron stuck his arm out and pushed two of them away from the others. "These are mine."

"I have to give it to you, Spring," David said. "Your hunch played out, and you sure do offer a guy interesting dates."

"Dates?" several voices said in unison as inquiring and incredulous gazes moved between Spring and the architect.

Blabbermouth, Spring thought.

The discovery of the stolen goods warehouse and the second downtown burglary, while not directly related, according to police, dominated the front-page reports in the next issue of the *Cedar Springs Gazette*. The fireworks from the planning commission meeting over the development plans was relegated to the third page.

The police chief's community meeting was moved from the multipurpose room at city hall to the auditorium at the high school to accommodate the crowd. And David returned to Charlotte to see to some business with his firm.

He and Spring talked almost every night and twice Spring read bedtime stories to Jeremy, her voice coming through speakerphone on David's mobile lulling the boy to sleep.

One evening David brought up the proverbial elephant in the room—in their deepening relationship.

"My team has drafted some plans, Spring. We'll be returning to Cedar Springs to present the options to city staff and the council. I wanted you to know ahead of time."

"I see," she said. "That was awfully fast."

"Spring, I'm telling you because I think you'll be pleased with what we've come up with. Driving around your land, hearing the stories about the city's history, those things helped me a lot."

"Gee, thanks," Spring said.

"Sarcasm doesn't suit you," he said.

That did it. "And how would you know what suits me, David?"

"Spring, you're upset…"

"Ya think?"

"This is why I wanted to have this conversation in person. I knew the phone was a mistake."

"Everything about this so-called relationship has been a mistake," she snapped back at him.

"Don't say that. You don't mean it. I know you don't."

Spring shook her head even though she knew he couldn't see her. "Goodbye, David."

"Spring, wait!"

She sighed. "What?"

"I really think you'll like what I've come up with."

She held the phone away from her ear as if he were talking in an ancient tongue. And then she did what she'd thought about doing from time to time with various people through the years. She hung up on him.

"So," Autumn Darling said as she worked out on the elliptical next to Spring's the next day. "I miss one cheesecake confab at Summer's only to discover that Winter's been dating a criminal and you've hooked up with the man trying to turn the farmhouse into a condo and fast-food development."

Spring groaned. This morning workout with her baby sister at F.I.T., the gym Autumn co-owned with two other fitness freaks, was supposed to be cathartic, not a source of more stress.

She wiped her brow with the small towel draped over her shoulder, then moved from the elliptical next to Autumn and onto a rowing machine.

"First, Winter is not seeing a criminal. It was two dates and she dumped him as soon as she figured it out. And for the record, I have not 'hooked up' with anyone."

"Well, whatever you old people call dating," Autumn said.

A dozen years separated the oldest Darling sibling from the youngest. And the dig about "old people" was a good-humored one that had been oft repeated through the years. Today, however, the barb hit home with uncharacteristic alacrity.

Spring stopped rowing and burst into tears.

Autumn was so startled she nearly fell off the elliptical.

"Oh, honey. I'm sorry," she said, rushing to her sister's side. "I didn't mean anything by that."

F.I.T. had not yet opened to the public for the day, so they were alone. Spring buried her head in the towel and wept as if her world had come undone at the first stroke of her oars.

Spring realized Autumn had never seen her big sister lose her cool. Autumn murmured comforting words and rubbed Spring's back until the sobs subsided into hiccups and then sniffles.

"Feel better?"

Spring nodded. "Sorry."

"Don't apologize for being human," Autumn said, squeezing her sister's shoulders.

"Help me out of this torture machine of yours."

Autumn did. Instead of heading to the showers, they walked to the marked lanes along the gym's interior perimeter that were used for walkers and indoor runners to do laps.

"I take it that jag wasn't about being old."

Spring sniffled and smiled. "What a perceptive child you are." After a minute or so of them walking in silence, Spring said, "Do you want kids, Autumn?"

"Crumb snatchers? Sure. But not now."

Spring gave a decidedly unladylike snort. "Take some advice from your big sister. Don't let 'not now' turn into 'it's too late.'"

"What's going on, Spring?"

The doctor squared her shoulders and increased her pace, which Autumn easily and quickly matched. "Just a little overdue introspection," she said. Then, "Let's turn this little stroll into some real exercise."

With that, she took off at a run, leaving a bemused Autumn to catch up or give up.

Spring didn't have a shift at Cedar Springs General Hospital that day. She was, however, scheduled at Common Ground. That's where the flowers were delivered.

The bouquet of mixed exotics was beautiful.

"Wow," Shelby, the clinic's front desk receptionist, said. "Aren't you the lucky one?"

Spring plucked the card from the floral pick in the blooms, read it and grimaced. "When the Common Ground messenger comes around today, please have him take these to Manna. Summer can use them for the dining room," she said to Shelby.

"Doc?" Shelby asked, concern lacing in her voice.

Spring shook her head and walked away from David's apology.

The next delivery hit her hard.

A large same-day FedEx envelope arrived. It had no return address, and she wondered how the sender had managed that. When she opened it, with Shelby looking on, she discovered a sheaf of papers. The one on top was a piece of cream-colored construction paper with multicolor crayon drawings completed in the style of a four-year-old child. The picture included three stick figures, two tall ones and a little one, all holding hands along with what looked like a brown snowman with a bow tie next to the little stick figure. A crookedly drawn red heart was in the corner of the page, presumably as a signature.

"Oh, Jeremy, sweetie. You're not playing fair, David," she whispered.

"What is it?" Shelby asked.

Spring glanced at the other papers in the envelope. She saw an embossed logo with "Carolina Land Associates" at the bottom of the page and jammed them back inside without further consultation. She held on to the construction paper drawing, though.

She passed Shelby the envelope. "Would you please see that these are shredded?"

"Shredded? But—"

Spring took the envelope back. "That's all right," she said. "I'll do it. When is my next appointment?"

Shelby glanced at the schedule and then gave Spring a quizzical look before answering.

"Not until two."

"Send any walk-ins my way," Spring requested as she headed to the volunteers' lounge with her drawing and FedEx envelope of unread documents.

"You're scaring your sister, and you're starting to scare me," Cecelia Jeffries told her best friend that night. She and Spring were at the Corner Café downtown, where Spring was pretending to eat half of a Cobb salad and Cecelia was acting in the role of older, wiser best friend and sister-confidant. Her multicolored reading glasses had polka dots on them and made Spring smile.

"I'm fine, CeCe."

"Uh-huh. You've dropped five pounds in a week and you're working like the end of the world is tomorrow."

"Maybe it is."

"Spring."

She pushed the salad aside. "He's showing the designs to the city council, and with that burglary warehouse being out at the farm, Bernadette has even more ammunition to take the property via eminent domain. We've put a lot of work into the grant application for the history center, but it was all a waste of time."

"How can you say that?"

"Because, CeCe, even if we get the grant, which we won't find out for another six weeks, by then it will be too late. This is yet another of the mayor's fast-track projects."

"Maybe we should go public with our plans for the land."

"You can if you'd like. I'm just tired of fighting."

Cecelia leaned back in her chair and regarded her friend. "You fell in love with him and you think he's betrayed you by continuing with his plans."

"Good deductive reasoning, Dr. Many Degrees. I see you've added psychology to your repertoire."

"That's *Professor* Many Degrees."

The little joke earned a small smile from Spring.

Cecelia cocked her head and raised her brow. "Wow, girl, you've got it bad."

Spring shook her head. "Not possible, CeCe. I just met the man. I know nothing about him. Well, nothing besides his job, his son and his mother."

Cecelia grinned. "People have married each other knowing far less. Face it, Spring, you've been struck by Cupid's arrow. Fallen in love at first sight. Found your soul mate and all that."

"Please. I'm not eighteen and starry-eyed."

"Nope," Cecelia said. "You're thirty-five and jaded."

"Speaking of being young and starry-eyed. I completely fell apart on Autumn today."

"I know," Cecelia said. "She called me. She's never, *ever* seen you cry. Did you know that? You were always the one wiping away tears, not shedding them. She said she thought about calling Lovie, but decided that would be like calling in the National Guard for something a meter maid could handle."

Spring closed her eyes. "Well, thank the Lord for small blessings. That's all I need is more questioning from my mother. I got an earful and then some out at the farmhouse after David and

I found that storage facility and he mentioned dating. You'd think I was the youngest the way they've all been acting."

"That's because you've been acting like a woman in love and they've never seen that before."

"Can we please talk about something else?"

"No," Cecelia said. "You have to face this thing."

"There is no thing."

"Then why did you give away a perfectly lovely arrangement of flowers from him and say you were going to shred everything he's sent you?"

Spring threw up her hands. "Spies are everywhere! Who are you, MI6?"

Cecelia reached across the table, grabbed one of Spring's hands and clutched it in her larger brown ones. "I'm your friend, Spring. Your best friend. I know the secrets your sisters and mother don't. I know why you're afraid, and, let me assure you, sister, it's time to let it go."

Spring felt water well up in her eyes and she swallowed back the tears. She would not cry. Not again.

"It's not supposed to be like this," she said. "It's not supposed to hurt or be so complicated."

"Says who? Girlfriend, if men weren't worth

the heartache, the human species would cease to exist. Marriages would crumble. Life as we know it—"

Spring snatched her hand away. "I get your point."

"That honey boy and his little man are worth fighting for."

"But he's fighting to take away something I love."

"He's forcing you to shift your paradigms, to consider new and alternative scripts for the same tired screenplay you've been reading since Keith."

Spring stared at her friend. She realized with a start and with sudden clarity that that was the first time she'd heard his name spoken aloud in a long time. While the ache of how he'd used, abused and lied to her remained, it was a vague sort of ache, like the distant memory of a fall or a bad tuna sandwich from a month ago. She didn't have to believe or accept that David might—or might not—be The One. But she could allow herself to be free of the past.

She may have been keeping her emotional self cloistered away and shielded from potential hurt, and Cecelia was right. It was time to let the ghost of Keith Henson float away.

"And the light shines through," Cecelia said.

"What?"

Cecelia smiled. "Your expression. Something just happened to you. I watched it cross your face."

Spring reached for her salad and picked up her fork.

"You, Professor Many Degrees, are way too perceptive. And I love you for it, my friend."

Chapter Thirteen

The conversation with Cecelia clarified Spring's thinking. Rather than resigning or conceding the battle, she discovered within her a new enthusiasm and will to make the history-center project a go.

She was a doctor, a pediatrician, but she could string coherent sentences together. She wasn't an editorial writer or journalist. Yet the idea of putting her thoughts and concerns on paper carried a certain appeal. It was easy to let her emotions get in the way when talking to David or to fail to find the words to express what she wanted to say when talking to her sisters. She knew she and David were not going to see eye to eye on this in a conversation. They were both too passionately invested in what each thought was the right course of action.

Writing an op-ed for the newspaper would

give her the opportunity to lay out her rationale and concerns in a cohesive way—without the distraction of his presence throwing her off-kilter. So she called the local paper and inquired about writing an op-ed column about the benefits and reasons for historic preservation.

At a maximum of 250 words, the letters to the editor were basically a few paragraphs of opinion. But the columns that ran opposite of the editorial page, hence op-ed, were much longer and gave the opportunity for a more thorough analysis of an issue. She also liked that there was no arguing back with the writer. If people disagreed, they had to write a letter to the editor, which had to be mailed, emailed or hand-delivered to the offices of the *Cedar Springs Gazette*.

Although she had nothing to lose and didn't know what to expect of her request, she was surprised when the editor not only liked the idea but offered her own twist: she would get someone to write a pro piece to Spring's con.

"You do understand that I envision these pieces running on the same day," Mac Scott, the editor of the *Cedar Springs Gazette* said.

Spring nodded. "Who is writing the pro piece?"

"I liked your idea. So after you called, I put out a couple of feelers, but I have no solid commitment yet," Mac said.

"I'm sure Mayor Howell would jump at the opportunity."

Mac shook her head. "My goal is to keep politics out of it. This is about community reaction and response."

Spring liked that. An elected official, by virtue of office, could be seen to have more sway than an ordinary citizen would.

"I'm looking forward to reading the other side's point of view."

Mac chuckled and pulled her hair back. "You and me both. I have to tell you, I had no idea how much this issue would resonate with people. On both sides."

"Selling a lot of papers?"

"Print circulation is about the same, but our website is going gangbusters."

Any arguments—and she knew David would have many to derail her solid case against the project—would have to be silenced in the short run. Cedar Springs City Council members and newspaper readers alike would only be able to read her words and contemplate her reasoning before offering up their own ideas and alternate opinions on the matter.

As a member of both the Darling family and of the Cedar Springs Historical Society, Spring knew more than most about the history of the city. But for something this important, she wouldn't rely on memory and emotion. This was a task that called for research and action.

She thanked Mac for the opportunity, then, after grabbing her purse and her laptop, she headed to the library. Information from the library's special collection of local and North Carolina history would be just what she needed to supplement her piece.

"Daddy, I want Seuss."

Jeremy and David, ensconced again in their home away from home, had just completed a cut-throat game of Go Fish. Jeremy had come out victorious and declared his prize.

"Go get it," David told him. "It's in your backpack."

"Nuh-uh," Jeremy said. "Grandma spilled chocolate milk. Seuss got wet."

David bit back a grin. "Grandma spilled the milk?"

Jeremy stuck his thumb in his mouth. His sure tell.

"Jeremy?" David put his own thumb in his mouth and pulled it out, showing Jeremy the action he wanted the boy to take. Jeremy would be headed to kindergarten next year, and David did not want his son's propensity to suck his thumb when stressed or fibbing to head to school with him.

The boy released his thumb and confessed. "Maybe I helped her spill a little bit."

That explained the alternate backpack that Jeremy had been toting when he transferred from Grandma Charlotte's car to David's.

This trip to Cedar Springs, David told himself, was just a little father-son overnight. But that wasn't true, and he knew it.

Spring had not returned his calls or text messages. And there had been nothing but silence from her after he'd sent both the flowers and his revised renditions for the site plans. He'd been so proud of the work he'd done on a compromise plan. He and his team had created it following the meetings with the city officials. Coupled with that was the knowledge he'd gained at the intervention by the Magnolia Supper Club and the appreciation he'd gotten for not only the Darling land, but all of the city parcels, after having roamed the length and breadth of the Darling homestead with Spring.

If not turn cartwheels, he thought she would at least express an appreciation for his effort.

"Can we go see my Spring?"

David started to say Spring didn't want to see them, but he reconsidered that and then studied his son. Somewhere along the way, Jeremy had stopped calling her Dr. Spring. She'd simply become *my* Spring.

Except for that one night.

They'd taken to calling each other around Jeremy's bedtime. Spring would help tuck Jeremy in via the phone. She'd purchased a copy of his favorite book about the train, the turtle and the boy, as well as a few other storybooks, and read them to him over the phone while David turned the pages on his end in Charlotte.

He had suggested a video call over a program like Skype, but the pediatrician said video stimulation before bed wasn't a good idea. Jeremy had a routine that worked, and sticking to it provided continuity. So they'd continued the calls, the stories, lullabies and prayers, falling into a routine that neither David nor Spring talked about. After the bedtime routine, he and Spring would talk for a bit. It was an odd relationship. Anyone looking at it from the outside would assume Spring was, like many in the region so close to Fayetteville and Fort Bragg, a deployed military mom maintaining the home ties while serving overseas.

And then, a few nights ago, Jeremy was drifting off. Spring had wished him a good-night and Jeremy murmured, "G'night, Mommy."

David wasn't sure he'd heard his son correctly, but then he clearly heard Spring's startled intake of breath and knew he had. Jeremy was knocked out, Beau at his side as he'd been from the day after his emergency surgery. When he took the phone off speaker and lifted it to his ear to talk to Spring, the connection was dead.

David stared at Jeremy. The boy was cute. That was for sure.

Irresistible?

David didn't know, but he wanted Spring Darling back in their lives any way he could accomplish it. And his pint-size buddy might be the answer.

He wasn't proud of the idea that sprouted in his head like a weed in an untended lawn. But Spring and her friends had run an intervention on him. Wasn't it fair turnabout for him and his son to return the favor?

The intercom buzzed in the volunteers' lounge at the Common Ground clinic. "Dr. Darling, you have visitors at the front desk."

Spring looked up from her laptop. She'd had a rush of patients and appointments earlier, but when things had slowed down, she'd opened the computer to work on her op-ed for the newspaper.

Former patients sometimes stopped by to let her know how they were doing or to update her on the situations that had been prayed over.

"My folks never come back to say hi," intoned one of the volunteers who came in twice each month to do general dentistry.

"It's the drills, Patrick," Spring said with a smile. "Just the memory of that sound gives people the heebie-jeebies."

"Just for that," he said, "you get the big one the next time you're in the chair."

Chuckling, she saved her document and closed the laptop, then slipped on her Common Ground lab coat.

She heard Jeremy's voice before she got to the lobby. He was proudly, and in the loud voice that only a four-year-old thinks is quiet, informing someone that he had a scar from the hospital. A pang of longing shot through her. She'd missed her little man. But hot on that thought was that if Jeremy was there, so, too, was his father. The Spring of a few days ago would have turned on her heel and proceeded with haste out the back door. The new Spring scoffed at such cowardice and instead boldly strode to meet the Camden men.

Her breath caught when she got sight of them, and her heart seemed to swell with a fullness that she would have found overwhelming had it not felt so good.

They'd not yet spotted her, and she soaked in just seeing them. They were dressed in identical outfits. Khaki pants, short-sleeve blue button-down shirts and sneakers. And they both looked as if they'd stopped at a salon for cuts and styling before coming to the clinic. Father and son sported trim but spiky hair that looked as if it had a mousse or gel in it. She grinned at their "me and mini-me" looks.

"This is for Spring," Jeremy announced. "I picked it out myself."

"I'm sure she'll love it," Shelby replied. She noticed Spring and added, "Well, look at who I see."

Jeremy whirled around and let out a whoop.

She was ready for the torpedo launch of his embrace and hugged him tight.

"I missed you. You didn't read me a story."

"I know, baby," she cooed. "I'm sorry. Did you get to sleep all right without me?"

Jeremy nodded. "Beau helped me."

"And where is Beau?"

"At the hotel. He couldn't get a haircut, so he had to stay there."

In the time she'd been talking with Jeremy, she'd felt David's eyes on her but hadn't looked at him. She feared that everything she felt for them would show on her face and in her eyes. But when Jeremy said *at the hotel*, her gaze lifted and met David's.

He was watching them with an intensity that made Spring unconsciously hold Jeremy even tighter. When he wiggled in her arms, she let him down.

"I picked out a flower for you," he said, thrusting a half-crushed pink carnation at her.

Although she knew it had little or no scent, she buried her nose in it to give her a moment to regroup. "It's beautiful, Jeremy. Thank you."

"Can I go to space station?"

"Sure," Spring and David answered at the same time.

She blushed. "I'm sorry."

"How about I show you what we've gotten since you were last here," Shelby said, taking the little boy's hand and giving Spring a conspiratorial wink.

"Hello, Spring."

She couldn't stall any longer. The time was now for the new Spring to let go of the past and face the future. She didn't know if the future for her held this man, but she wanted to find out.

"Hi, David."

And the next thing she knew, she was in his arms.

Spring didn't know—or care—who moved first. She just soaked in the warmth and strength and rightness of the moment.

"I missed you, too," he murmured in her hair.

"Oh, David." His name was longing and hope tinged with despair.

When she pulled away from the embrace, she wiped at her moist eyes.

"What are you doing here? Is it time for your meeting with the city council?"

He gave her an odd look. "That's not until next week. We just came for the weekend because Jeremy—because I wanted to see you."

Spring's smile was tremulous. "How did you know I'd be here?"

"It seemed like the best place to begin," he said. "If you weren't here, the hospital would have been the next stop. And then the farmhouse. And since I don't know where you live, if you weren't there, either, I was going to call Cameron Jackson."

"I'm easy to find," she said. "The phone book."

"Ah, old-school technology. It never crossed my mind."

She shook her head in amusement. "You two hit it off, huh?"

"Chief Cam? Yeah, he's a stand-up kind of guy."

This time she did chuckle. "Everyone says that about him. And using exactly those same words. I don't exactly know what it means, being a stand-up kind of guy, but he makes my sister happy and that's all that matters to me."

He took her hand in his. "I'd like to matter to you, Spring Darling, to make you happy."

Chapter Fourteen

She didn't get to respond because the front doors burst open and a group of people running and shouting tumbled in. A man had a bleeding girl in his arms, a woman and an older woman were both wailing in Spanish.

"*Médico, por favor! Médico.* We need doctor. Somebody help us."

"Shelby! Patrick!" Spring hollered as she jumped into action. She pulled gloves from her pocket and snapped them on. "What happened?"

"*La cortadora de césped. Un accidente! Un accidente!*" another man with the group kept saying. He was drenched in sweat and was alternating between crying out and looking as if he may pass out.

Spring's Spanish was rudimentary. All she got out of that was that it was an accident.

"I'm a doctor," she said. She tapped her chest and said, *"Médico."*

The girl had cuts all across her legs. Spring couldn't determine from what. All she knew was that they needed to stop the bleeding first, get her hooked up to an IV and transported to the hospital as quickly as possible.

"It was a lawn mower accident," David said.

Spring glanced at him with gratitude. "You speak Spanish?" When he nodded, she said, "Thanks."

At that moment, Patrick came on the run with a gurney.

Shelby was already on the phone with the emergency department at Cedar Springs General and ordering an ambulance.

David got out of the way and watched the small volunteer medical crew work. At the same moment he turned to look for Jeremy, he felt a tug on his pants leg.

"Daddy?"

He lifted a wide-eyed Jeremy into his arms and turned him away from the bloody scene and the noise of frantic parents and relatives.

"She's hurt."

"Yeah, buddy."

Jeremy twisted around, trying to get a look at what was happening, but David carried him toward the children's waiting room, hoping that the toys and colors would distract him.

"Spring is gonna make her better."

Jeremy said it with such assurance that all David could do was nod.

Jeremy sat on his lap. "Daddy, we need to pray for her."

Out of the mouths of babes, David thought.

So he and Jeremy prayed for the girl and for her family and for the medical team working to get her stabilized. Not too much later, they heard an ambulance.

Jeremy ran for the door, wanting to go see, but David caught him and held him back.

"She's going to the hospital, buddy. More doctors need to help her."

"My hospital with Dr. Emmanuel? He made me better, too."

He didn't know the extent of the girl's injuries, or if the little hospital in Cedar Springs would be where they took her or if they would airlift her to Durham and to the trauma center at Duke University Hospital. To his untrained eye, her injuries had looked horrendous. And he knew firsthand the panic and fear that her parents now faced.

"I don't know, buddy. It will depend on how badly she's hurt."

Jeremy considered that for a moment, then quietly asked, "Can we go see her?"

David looked at his son, who was now sitting in a little chair that had wheels and resembled a Formula One race car like his bed at home. "Who?"

"The girl."

Floored, David didn't know what to say. After a moment, he came up with a plausible response for his son. "We'll ask Spring about that, okay?"

Jeremy nodded, then scooted across the room to a toy box.

Almost a full hour passed before Spring appeared in the entryway of the waiting room. She'd clearly washed up and changed clothes because she now wore slacks and a white cotton shirt.

David rose and went to her. "Is she okay?"

"Still in surgery at Cedar Springs General. Where's…"

Before she got the rest of the question out, she spotted Jeremy. He'd fallen asleep on the little sofa in front of the DVD. Her mouth curved up in a smile and then dismay.

"He saw?"

David nodded. "He wants to go see her. The girl."

"Her name's Maria," Spring said, pinching the bridge of her nose and then rolling each shoulder as if trying to get the kinks out. "Maria de Silva. She's six. I'll check with the hospital later to see how she's doing."

David glanced at Jeremy. "Thank you. He's really worried about her."

"Our little man has lots of compassion."

David glanced at her sharply, but her focus was on Jeremy.

Our little man. He wondered if she meant that literally or figuratively.

Jeremy had made it clear on more than one occasion, both lucid and drowsy, that he wanted Spring to be his mom.

David wanted the same thing and could think of nothing better in his life than Spring agreeing to be his wife and the two of them raising Jeremy and any other children who came along. He knew, however, that they had a long way to go emotionally as a couple before marriage and the long term could be considered. And there was still the business of the development project between them.

He was trying to figure out what to say to her, when Spring took his hand.

"David, I know this is going to sound strange. I want to—no, I need to clear my head and just…" She shrugged. "I don't know, just be. Would you mind terribly if we got out of here? Can the three of us just go somewhere to do something fun?"

He smiled and lifted her hand to press a kiss to it. "I like the way you think, Dr. Darling."

Not only did Spring want to do something fun, she had something specific in mind.

"This weekend is Common Ground's community picnic," she told him after Jeremy was buckled in his car seat and she and David settled in front. "I wasn't planning to go to any of the Friday events, but I think it would be perfect."

"What's on tap?" David asked as he started his SUV.

"All three of the Common Ground churches are hosting events this weekend. The Chapel of the Groves is showing family films all day with all the popcorn you can eat and some musical entertainment between the features. The Chapel of the Groves is Cecelia's church. Tomorrow, at my church, First Memorial, there's a picnic and bazaar, then fireworks later in the evening. And on Sunday, The Fellowship has services and puppet shows and carnival games."

"Sounds fun. Are you sure you're up for it?"

"Most definitely." To emphasize her point, she twisted around to look at Jeremy. "Want to go to the movies?"

"Yes!"

Spring sat back and glanced at David. "It's all settled. Two votes for the movies."

"Can we go to the hospital and see the girl?"

David and Spring shared a glance.

"The doctors are with her right now," Spring said.

"Dr. Emmanuel?"

"I don't know, Jeremy," she said. "But that's a good guess. He's a very good surgeon."

"I know," the boy said in a tone that was a bit too wise for his years.

"Tell you what," Spring said. "I'll see what I can find out after our movie. Okay?"

"Okay," Jeremy said, once again sounding like a four-year-old. He stuck his thumb in his mouth and stared out the window.

Watching in the rearview mirror, David looked at his son but didn't say or do anything about the thumb-sucking. Under the circumstances, the gesture seemed a comfort. David reached for his own comfort, clasping Spring's hand with his free one. She squeezed it lightly, then gave him directions to the Chapel of the Groves.

Jeremy fell asleep three-fourths of the way through the movie about talking cars. He lay curled on his side, his head in Spring's lap.

"Any word yet?" David asked when he saw her reach for her phone.

"Just checking now," she said. "He's really worried about her. He asked me again about her condition."

David ran a hand along his son's brow. "I've never seen him like this before. It's like he went from a little boy to a grown man."

"He knows some of what she's feeling," Spring said. "While he didn't have the type of injuries Maria has, he knows—whether consciously or unconsciously—that she's in pain and probably very scared."

"It puts things into perspective, doesn't it?"

Spring nodded. "It sure does."

The report about Maria de Silva that came in the next morning from the hospital was a good one. David gave Jeremy the news over breakfast in the hotel's lobby. Jeremy made one request as he started out of the hotel's parking lot to pick up Spring.

David glanced at his son in the rearview mirror. "Sure, buddy. We can do that."

Then, following the directions she'd given him, David made his way to Spring's house. She was watering a flower bed when they rolled up and walked toward her.

"I wanna help," Jeremy said eyeing the water coming out of the hose in a streaming arc.

"Good morning," she said. "Well, let's put you to work, then."

David watched in amusement as she guided him on where to spray the hose. Jeremy giggled as he got the hang of it with her help on the nozzle.

He hauled a bag of mulch to them and watched as Spring showed Jeremy how to spread it in the small flower beds after weeding.

"I see you finally found a helper for the garden."

David recognized the voice and tensed.

Today was supposed to be a day of no stress, a respite from arguing about architectural renderings, land use or historic preservation. Yet there stood one of the chieftains of the opposition. She was dressed casually in capri pants and a smock with pockets and had a floppy straw hat on her head.

He straightened, dusted off his hands and said, "Hello, Mrs. Darling."

Lovie Darling looked him up and down, and then she sighed. "Good morning, Mr. Camden." The tone was civil if not warm. "And who is this?" she asked, bending toward Jeremy, who was now tugging on a weed in a small bed of colorful flowers. The weed was winning the battle against the boy.

"Mother, this is Mr. Camden's son, Jeremy."

"Hi," Jeremy said. "It's stuck."

"Let me show you a little trick," Lovie Darling said. She produced a pair of gardening shears and told Jeremy to watch as she made the cut.

"When you do it here," she told him, holding the pesky weed at the base of the plant and burrowing a bit in the soil, "you get more of the root. You won't get it all, but it will take a little while before you have to weed again."

"What's your name?" Jeremy asked.

"You, my dear, may call me Lovie."

With the four-year-old as her assistant, Lovie Darling cleared the small patch of three additional weeds while both a bemused Spring and an amused David looked on.

After a quick washup to get the dirt off hands and Jeremy's face, Spring tucked a wicker basket and blanket on the rear seat of the vehicle. Then she, Jeremy and David were on the way to the bazaar and picnic. And Jeremy had a date to meet up with Lovie later at the church.

"If I hadn't seen it with my own eyes, I wouldn't have believed it," Spring said.

David chuckled. "After that planning commission meeting, I think I'll have to agree. It's the power of the cute kid."

When David made the wrong turn, Spring pointed out that First Memorial Church of Cedar Springs was in the opposite direction of where they were headed.

"But Cedar Springs General is this way," he said.

"Are we there yet?" Jeremy called from the backseat.

"Almost, buddy."

Spring raised her eyebrows, but David just smiled.

The Camden men led the way as if they, instead of Spring, worked at the hospital. She went with them, pausing briefly at the patient visitor desk.

"What's in the bag?" she asked David as they rode the elevator to the third floor of the hospital.

"Something Jeremy bought."

Her mouth curved up. "Jeremy bought?"

"Well, Jeremy picked out and Dad's plastic paid for."

"It's a surprise," Jeremy said, practically hopping on his toes in anticipation.

"I think I know where we're going," she said in a low voice to David.

He laced her fingers with his as the doors swooshed open and Jeremy dashed out. "I think you'd be right," he said. "To the right, Jeremy."

The boy paused and looked both ways, then turned and looked up at his father.

"Face forward, the way we are," David said. Jeremy turned so his back was to them. "Now remember what we learned about the heart."

"Yes!" Jeremy placed his hand on his chest as if about to recite the Pledge of Allegiance or sing the National Anthem at a ball game. "My heart is on my left, so we go that way," he exclaimed pointing down the correct hallway.

"Good job, buddy. We're looking for room number three-zero-six. You think you can find that?"

Jeremy nodded and walked slowly down the corridor, peering up at the room numbers and calling them out as individual digits as he went.

"Very creative," Spring complimented David.

He grinned. "I know the heart is really—"

She held up her free hand, stopping him. "That lesson is a perfect way to teach a young child about right and left. And look," she said. "He's found the room."

Jeremy stood outside Room 306, waving for them to hurry up. "I need my bag," he said in a loudish whisper.

David handed the medium-size shopping bag to the boy. "Remember what we talked about now."

Jeremy nodded and bit his lip as if suddenly unsure about his plan.

"It's all right, buddy," David said, releasing Spring's hand and taking his son's. He knocked on the partially open door.

Spring knew that Jeremy had been worried about the little girl. That David had followed through and actually brought him to the hospital to see her said a lot about both of them.

A dark-haired woman appeared at the door and looked up at David. He said something in rapid Spanish, and her face blossomed into a welcoming smile. She ushered them in, talking the entire time. David quietly and efficiently translated for Spring and Jeremy.

"Thank you so much for allowing us to visit," he told Mrs. de Silva. "As I mentioned on the phone, Jeremy was a patient here a few weeks ago. And after seeing Maria at the Common Ground clinic, he's been very worried about her."

"She is doing much better, all praise be to God," Mrs. de Silva said. "We have not stopped praying."

"Neither have we," David told her.

"Daddy."

He smiled down at Jeremy.

"We won't disturb you long," he told the woman.

Mrs. de Silva smiled at Jeremy. Then, taking his free hand, she led him to the bed where little Maria was bandaged and looking miserable. She turned from the muted television and looked at them.

David made the introductions. Mrs. de Silva's eyes widened when she realized who Spring was.

"Thank you for helping my Maria," she said, giving Spring a hug.

At the girl's bedside, Jeremy reached into the bag and pulled out a white plush teddy bear. It wore a pink-and-green-polka-dot scarf around its neck. The girl's face lit up when she saw it.

"You need a bear," he told Maria, thrusting the toy at her. "It will make you feel better. I was sick and got Beau. You have to give her a name."

She wasn't able to move the lower part of her body, but she held tight to the teddy bear.

"Amelie," she said. *"Su nombre es Amelie. Gracias."*

Mrs. de Silva gasped, and David asked what was wrong.

"She has named the bear Amelie. Amelie was her best friend. She moved away a year ago." Tears filled the woman's eyes, and she wiped them away with a handkerchief she pulled from a pocket. "The two, my Maria and her friend Amelie, had matching pink-and-green dresses. She has missed her friend very much. Your little boy has made her very happy. Thank you."

Watching from a few steps away, Spring covered her mouth, overcome by Jeremy's sensitivity and concern and the Lord putting them all in the right places at the right times.

Despite the language barrier, Jeremy and Maria seemed to be enjoying each other's company. David eventually had to remind him that Maria needed rest just like he had after his tummy surgery.

"Would you let us pray with you before we leave?" David asked.

"Sí," Mrs. de Silva said. "And please pray for my brother. He is very upset about what has happened. It was an accident, but he blames himself. My husband and I have tried to tell him it was not his fault, but..." She shook her head sadly.

"Of course we will," David said. He held a hand out to Spring. The three adults formed a semicircle around the bed. Jeremy put his hand on Maria's arm, and David led them in prayer.

Back in the SUV, Spring twisted in her seat and told Jeremy, "What you did for Maria was very nice."

He nodded. "She needed a bear. But she should call it Beau."

Spring smiled.

David started the sport utility vehicle and announced, "Next stop, the bazaar and picnic."

Spring had initially thought that it would be all right for David and Jeremy to meet her at the picnic. But as David followed the direction of an usher managing traffic in the church's parking lot, she was glad that he'd insisted they would pick her up at her house.

Not only had her mother seen David in a light other than as adversary, she'd met and seemed as smitten with Jeremy as Spring was. And then the stop at the hospital. David had clearly followed through and had even talked with Maria de Silva's mother in advance of their visit.

She couldn't think of a more perfect day, and it had barely gotten started for them.

Jeremy's enthusiasm was contagious. He practically vibrated in his booster seat in the backseat of David's SUV.

David parked at First Memorial Church of Cedar Springs.

In the backseat, Jeremy bounced in his seat and pointed out the window.

"Look, look, it's a clown! He's throwing balls!"

The colorful clown juggler, much like a pied piper, was walking around, pausing to hold court as people arrived in the parking lot and then leading them toward the festivities.

"Hurry, Daddy! We're going to miss him!"

David and Spring shared a smile.

"He'll be here all day, buddy."

Jeremy's feet kicked the seat as he squirmed.

"Many kids Jeremy's age are afraid of clowns," Spring quietly observed.

David grinned. "Not my boy. So far, about the

only thing I've discovered that he's afraid of is going to bed."

Spring laughed as David cut the engine. "My mom used to say that my youngest sister, Autumn, was like that. Too afraid she would miss something."

"That's Jeremy."

"Daddy, can we get out now?"

"On my way, buddy." David got out of the SUV, came around and opened Spring's door for her, then opened the back door to release Jeremy.

"Hurry, Daddy."

"I'm hurrying," David said with a smiling glance over his shoulder at Spring.

He undid the restraints, and Jeremy bounded from the booster seat and into his arms.

David glanced at Spring. "This was really a great idea," he told her. "I'm glad you invited us."

As he put Jeremy down, Spring reached across the backseat to the small picnic basket filled with cookies to share. "I'm glad you decided to come. This picnic is a First Memorial tradition. It's a lot of fun. It was incorporated into the full Common Ground community picnic weekend and has just gotten better every year. And," she added with a nod toward Jeremy, "it seems to have gotten his mind off Maria."

Jeremy grabbed his father's hand and Spring's free one to tug them forward.

Spring was struck by the image the three of them made.

They looked like a family.

And it felt right, so very right.

While Jeremy chattered between them about the fun they would have at the church picnic, Spring stole a glance at David…and caught him staring at her.

She wondered if he was thinking the same thing.

"This feels right," David said.

She didn't cast her gaze away, and she didn't feign either indifference or misunderstanding.

It did feel right. The way things were supposed to feel between a man and a woman.

"Yes," she told him. "It does."

The next two hours were spent going from booth to booth at the picnic. Each of the church's auxiliary groups had tents set up along the perimeter of the church's lawn. Each booth featured a game or activity, and there was something for people of all ages. Picnic tables laden with food and big barbecue grills were in the middle.

While the children watched a puppet show, a preview of what was to come the next day at The Fellowship, David and Spring signed up to play a round of Bible trivia.

The picnic and bazaar, while hosted by First Memorial, was open to all of the Common

Ground community so there were plenty of faces from the three congregations who were meeting for the first time.

"Remember," the host dressed in a tweed jacket said using the hyper voice of a television game show host. "You must answer each trivia item in the form of a question. And remember, if you don't, the points automatically go to your opposing team."

Two teams of four stood facing each other, the men versus the women. They were on opposite teams, and Spring wondered if David had any idea how competitive she could be. She waved at him and grinned. He was about to find out.

"You're going down," a tall man on the other side taunted.

"That may be the case," the brunette woman next to Spring responded. Spring couldn't remember if she'd introduced herself as Marcy Marian or Marian Marcy. Marcy or Marian then pulled out a tangle of keys and shook them. "Just remember who got you here and who has the keys to the car and house."

That rejoinder earned laughter from all the competitors.

Twenty questions later, the men looked stunned to have been defeated by the team of women, who'd broken out into an impromptu cheer led by Marian.

"I was head cheerleader in high school down in Fayetteville," she said as each of the four women collected an envelope from the moderator.

"Congratulations, ladies. Each of you wins a gift card for a free book from the Common Ground Bible bookstore and two free pastries at Sweetings. Whether or not you decide to share with those losers over there is your business."

"Hey," Marian's husband said, approaching with the men. "They had a ringer on their team. She teaches Sunday school."

"And if you came sometime," the teacher replied, "maybe you would have known some of the answers."

"Don't be a sore loser," Marian said as she linked her arm with her husband's. "If memory serves correctly—and it does—you were the main one advocating men versus women."

"That's right," David said as he joined Spring. He slipped his hand into hers. "The rest of us wanted to go mixed doubles."

"You're just saying that now so you don't sleep on the sofa tonight," one of his teammates said, slapping David on the back.

Spring's face flamed, and David sputtered. "We're not—"

The sharp clanging of cowbells interrupted his dissent.

It was a call to arms for teams in old-fashioned

family games like a three-legged race and corn hole, which involved tossing small beanbags into holes on an elevated platform and board.

Lovie Darling made good on her promise to meet Jeremy at the picnic, and the two teamed up for a tiny tikes and partner beanbag toss that ended up being more competitive for the kids than the adults' version was. She remained civil but not warm to David, and, like several others at the picnic, she eyed her daughter and the architect with more than passing curiosity and confusion.

After the games, the ministers of the Common Ground churches, directed by Reverend Dr. Joseph Graham of First Memorial Church, led the combined members of the congregations and their guests in grace and a fellowship song on the lawn.

By the time Spring and David settled on the blanket she'd brought with heaping plates from the serving tables, Jeremy had dozed off.

"Poor little guy," Spring said, brushing hair along his forehead. "He's all tuckered out."

"He's had a full day," David said. "I'm beginning to think fireworks will go on without us tonight."

Spring sat cross-legged with her plate in her lap and cut a small piece of barbecued chicken.

David was reaching for his own plate when his mobile phone buzzed in his pocket. He put the plate on the blanket and pulled it out to glance at the display. The number had a 919 area code. Cedar Springs. Since it was Saturday afternoon, Spring was with him and his mother would have used her own cell with its Charlotte area code, he got a bad feeling about the call.

"Excuse me," he told Spring. "I need to take this."

She nodded, and he answered but didn't get up to leave to take the call in private.

The caller on the other end was Gloria Reynolds, the Cedar Springs City Council clerk.

"Mr. Camden," she said, "so sorry to disturb you on the weekend. I tried your office yesterday and they said you'd already left for the day and were out of town."

"No problem, Ms. Reynolds," he said. "What can I do for you?"

Spring mouthed "Gloria?" and he nodded. She put her plate of chicken, baked beans and chips to the side and watched him.

"Something has come up having to do with your plans for the multi-use development," Gloria said. "Can you be at city hall at eight o'clock Monday for a meeting?"

David's mind raced with possibilities—none of them good. The first being that if a call from

Cedar Springs had come in to his office in Charlotte, his team would have immediately notified him whether he was in the office, down the hall or on the moon. While the planning commission had approved his work, their vote was simply a recommendation to the city council. The elected body, not the appointed one, had the final say and authority to enter into binding agreements with firms like his.

"That's not a problem at all," he told Gloria Reynolds. He knew not to ask a single yes-or-no question when trying to ferret out information. So his question to her was short and to the point. "What's changed with the project?"

"Just some developments the mayor wants to keep you abreast of with regard to your proposal."

David didn't like the sound of that at all. What would prompt an unscheduled meeting first thing Monday morning, not to mention a Saturday off-city-hours telephone call to tell him and what he believed to be fiction about calling Carolina Land Associates on Friday?

He tried, unsuccessfully, to glean additional information from the clerk, but she was close-mouthed and circumspect in what she said.

With a grimace, he pocketed the phone.

"What's wrong?" Spring immediately asked.

"I don't know," he told her. "There's been a special meeting called about the plans."

Spring shrugged. "I wouldn't be too concerned. It could be anything." Then, after a beat, she added, "With luck, it will be to cancel the whole thing."

He took the dig in the spirit in which it had been made. "Smarty-pants."

Spring grinned.

David could spend the rest of this otherwise perfect summer day wondering and worrying about what was going on, or he could enjoy his time with this beautiful woman.

"So," she said. "You never told me to what I owe this surprise weekend visit by the Camden men?"

"I told you," he said. "I missed you and wanted to see you."

He was not at all sure what she might say about his candor, but it was out now.

She opened her mouth. Closed it. Opened it again and then her shoulders slumped a bit.

Seeing her struggle and not wanting to hear a rejection, he reached for his plate and a knife and fork. "So, what did you think about my modifications?"

Like him, Spring had taken the moment to study her food. She cut another bit of chicken from the bone. "Modifications?" she asked before sampling the succulent meat.

"To the renderings. I sent them to you with Jeremy's drawing."

At the mention of the boy's name, her hand went to his back, where she lightly rested it. David watched as her cheeks flushed, giving her fair complexion a rosy glow.

"What?" he asked.

"I didn't read them," she said. "Actually, I tossed them. I meant to shred the packet. Except for Jeremy's drawing. I kept that. I think I tossed the rest in the back of the car."

He stared at her openmouthed for a moment, then caught himself and let out a small sigh. "Well," he said. "I suppose I should be grateful I didn't send originals."

Spring gave up on the food and placed her plate on the blanket. "David, this is something we need to get over or beyond for anything between us to work. But I'm not at all sure that it's something I *can* get past. And believe me—I've tried. What you're doing fundamentally changes what my family has worked for and maintained for close to two hundred years. Two centuries, David. That's a long time to maintain a trust. Through the years, we've sold or given away parcels of land, always for a purpose that advanced the city in some way."

She sighed and looked him directly in the eye. "What you're working on is a commercial development," she said. "A project that benefits not the city of Cedar Springs or its residents but the profit margin of the entities that will develop the land."

"Spring—"

"Hear me out, please. This is important to me."

When he nodded and put his plate next to hers on the blanket, she continued.

"In your presentation, you noted that a nature trail abuts the city-owned acreage. Do you know why that trail is there?"

"A parks and recreation department effort to get people outside to enjoy nature, get some fresh air instead of staying cooped up with video games and flat-screen televisions?"

She smiled. "Something like that."

"Out with it," he said. "You're clearly just dying to set me straight on something."

"Actually, I'm not. Dying to tell you, I mean. I do want you to know, though," Spring said. "I want you to know and understand so you'll get a better perspective on why it means so much, why people are so passionate."

"Passionate. That's one word to describe your friend at the meeting."

"Georgina tends to get a bit carried away,"

she said. "Nevertheless, there's a reasoning behind it."

"You donated the land and built the trail?"

"Not quite. My father did. The city promised a bike and nature trail that had been discussed ad nauseam, voted on and approved. They had good intentions, the city council and staff at the time, but lacked the resources ultimately needed to make it come to fruition. Things deteriorated, and there were some very bad feelings around town. My dad stepped in and made an alternate proposal. What resulted was an eight-mile trail that's used by the Cedar Springs residents who initially called for it, by elementary and middle school science teachers, by master naturalist and master gardener groups, by the running and walking clubs—"

"I get it, Spring."

"It's not just the Darling land that I'm concerned about," she said, rushing on before he could say anything else.

David knew she was ramping up for another round of public good versus private profits. The big "however" in the equation was that she didn't have an office of twenty people depending on her to keep a business in operating cash flow.

Carolina Land Associates had plenty of small contracts that were both rewarding to work on professionally and that were profitable for the firm. But not profitable enough to support a full-time staff of twenty, plus interns and part-time contractors. He'd worked hard to build the company. The thought that it could all be taken away wasn't something he wanted to contemplate.

"Spring, I wish you'd have taken a look at those modified plans. They incorporated a lot of what you and your friends told me about the city. And they can scale to any size parcel, including the ones already owned by the city."

"There'd be no need for a land grab?"

He shook his head and hoped that the denial was true.

Just like the Cedar Springs planning commission, he could only make recommendations. Ultimately, it would be a compromise between and among what the city wanted, what the eventual developer wanted and what residents and land-owners would accept. Part of his deal with the city would be that Carolina Land Associates was brought on board with whichever development company or companies were used for each phase of the project. It was how he could ensure future work for the firm and his people.

"We're talking a five-to eight-year build out," he said. "There would be three or four phases, each taking as much as two years to complete."

Jeremy stirred and said, "Daddy?"

As one, Spring and David turned to see Jeremy sitting up and rubbing his eyes.

"Hey, buddy."

"I'm hungry. Is it time for fireworks?"

Chapter Fifteen

When Spring arrived home that night, there were several voice messages and texts on her phone, a device she'd put on mute the entire day. After the first two demanding to know what was going on between her and *that man*, she tossed the phone on her dresser and headed to the shower to contemplate just that.

Among the things on her mind: the feeling of rightness she'd experienced the entire day, as if she had the family she'd always thought she'd have by this point in her life. Being mistaken for husband and wife at the Bible trivia game had been embarrassing...and comforting.

She turned the water on and let it and her complicated thoughts tumble around her.

At their hotel, David got a sleeping Jeremy into bed and made sure Beau the teddy bear was nearby in case he reached for it during the night. He'd made it through the fireworks, and he'd spent the drive to Spring's house chattering the entire time about the pyrotechnic show. He'd finally succumbed to sleep on the way to their hotel.

David stared down at his son and contemplated what the boy had said after they'd seen Spring to her door and safely inside.

"She's the mommy I always wanted, Daddy. Let's marry her."

Things were so simple when you were four, David thought.

Things got even more complicated Monday morning.

Spring was doing rounds at the hospital when she received a bizarre text from Cecelia.

911. Call me. 911.

Unlike Gerald Murphy, Cecelia wasn't given to fits of hysteria, and in all the years they'd known each other she'd never communicated a message like that. Spring's heart raced. Something had happened to her mother or to one of her sisters. Nothing else would explain such a message.

Before going to her next patient, she slipped into a staff room and called Cecelia.

"What's wrong? Is Lovie—"

Cecelia got to the point. "Your mother is fine. Your boyfriend isn't. Mayor Howell has a counteroffer from a big DC-area firm. They build tourist malls and hotels and want to bring something the size of Potomac Mills to Cedar Springs."

"What?"

"You heard me."

"But—"

"But get over here as soon as you can."

Cecelia rang off, and Spring stood there holding her phone.

She'd heard the words, but they made little sense. Potomac Mills was the largest outlet mall in Virginia and was one of the state's biggest tourist attractions. The mall itself had more than two hundred stores, not to mention the dozens of shopping centers and big-box businesses and retailers, hotels and restaurants that sprouted around the complex in a three-hundred-sixty-degree circle. There were brochures and seminars on how to navigate the "neighborhoods" that made up the mall. Bus tour groups dumped shoppers there for day trips. She and her sisters had made the trek north to the literal shop 'til you drop destination for weekend forays on more than one occasion.

Spring's breath caught.

The eight o'clock meeting. That had to have been the reason it had been called. To tell David that he not only had competition but that the competitor was Goliath.

Suddenly, even his original proposal didn't seem so bad. A few houses, some condos and some walk-to businesses. But this, this was a game changer. The mayor didn't just want to bring development to Cedar Springs. She wanted to change the entire character of the city, to make it a tourist destination instead of a suburban community of commuters, retirees and young professionals.

When she finally arrived at Cecelia's house, she wasn't surprised to find the executive committee of the historical society pacing holes in the professor's floors. She was, however, stunned to find David there.

Cecelia got her up to speed on what had transpired while Spring was at work.

"David's shared with us his plan for Heritage Township. Carol has drafted petitions for city residents and county residents to sign in opposition. Meredith said she's awaiting our word on any legal action we want to take. Gerald is stretched out in the guest room with one of his migraines. Maddie has been finding excuses to take tea to him."

Spring's head reeled, so she glommed on to just one of the bits of information. "Heritage Township? I thought he said—"

"Had you read, instead of destroying, those plans he sent you, you would have discovered that he'd altered them, considerably."

Spring turned toward David, who was talking with a couple of historical society members across the room. As if feeling her gaze on him, he looked up at her, lifting a brow in question.

"Tell me about this Heritage Township, CeCe."

As Cecelia was giving her the details, Cecelia's front-door chimes sounded.

"Someone get that," she called from the dining room table, where David's plans were spread and the three of them talked.

A moment later, Police Chief Zachary Llewelyn entered the dining room.

"Sorry to interrupt your meeting, folks, but Annette at the antiques store told me I could find all of you here."

Maddie Powers popped her head into the room. "Wait, Chief. I'll go wake Gerald."

When everyone was gathered around Cecelia's dining room table, the chief gave them his news.

"We've made a break in the burglary case."

"You recovered our items?" Gerald said.

Llewelyn nodded. "One of the suspects decided that the heat was getting a little too hot and told us everything. We found the things from Step Back in Time at a house on Elmhurst Street. We've had the property under surveillance for some time now. Our suspect also mentioned the warehouses the crew was using."

"At the farm?" Spring asked.

"And a couple of other locations," the police chief said. "I'm not at liberty to discuss the details of the case, but I wanted to personally let you know that we're making arrests and closing in on all of the suspects."

"When can we claim our pieces?"

"I'm sorry, but it will be a while," Chief Llewelyn said. "It's evidence at the moment."

"It's a blessing it was recovered, Gerald," Maddie Powers said.

The antiques dealer looked at her as if just seeing her for the first time. Then he smiled and patted her hand. "Yes. Yes, it is."

"What about the things taken from the art gallery?" Spring asked.

"Also recovered," Llewelyn said.

"This is great news," Gerald said. "Thank you, Chief."

The police chief nodded. "Well, if the rumors at city hall are true, you all have quite a situation on your hands. So I'll leave you to your meeting."

Cecelia offered him some coffee cake, which he took to go. When Cecelia returned to her dining room, Spring and David were alone and facing each other. She smiled and headed to the living room, where the rest of her guests were.

"I'm sorry I didn't read what you sent," Spring said.

David shrugged. "That's all right. It may not even matter now."

"It matters," she said, touching his arm.

"My company needed this contract," he said. He told her about the firm's precarious situation. "It's not in danger of going under, but I feel an obligation to provide for my employees. Laying off half of them is untenable."

"It doesn't have to be that way."

Spring wasn't sure exactly when and how she'd come to the realization, but she loved this man.

She blinked. Had she really just been stunned and blindsided by her own thoughts?

Loved?

Loved.

She'd tried to fight it. Tried to claim their differences were too great to overcome. But the obstacles had been made of smoke and fears with no basis in reality.

Spring wanted to know where this unlikely

relationship was going. She had run hot and cold when it came to David. In the beginning, she thought he was a homeless man just trying to get care for his son. Then she'd discovered he was here in Cedar Springs to destroy the one thing she loved the most.

Over time, she'd come to realize that there was more to David, so much more, including a strong but quiet faith like her own, a value system that put integrity first and, on top of it all, a deep and abiding love for his son.

She didn't think it was possible, but she'd fallen head over heels in love with David Camden. And Jeremy... The little boy had stolen her heart from the first. She was having a hard time envisioning her life without both of them in it.

The thought actually frightened her. She'd given her heart to a man just once before. And he'd returned her unconditional love with a betrayal that still stung fifteen years after the fact. David wasn't anything like Keith Henson, who'd wanted not her heart but her family's money. Comparing them would be like comparing a birthday party to after-school detention.

"What do you mean?" he asked.

Spring pulled one of the chairs out and sat, tugging him into its twin.

Instead of answering his question, she asked one of his own. "What happened to Jeremy's mother?"

He mouth curved up in a bittersweet smile. "I wondered when you'd ask that."

"I've wondered since the first night we met."

"Katy died," he said. "Jeremy was barely six months old when she was diagnosed with ovarian cancer. She was gone before he turned one."

"I'm sorry."

"I didn't think I would ever find a love like the one we had," he said. "I thought my world had ended. My mother moved in and eventually made me go back to work. She dragged me and Jeremy to church, to meals and into life again. When I met you, it was like storm clouds had dissipated and the sun again shone bright and beautiful. You were that sun, Spring. Jeremy and I love you. I love you. Would you do me the honor of being my wife and Jeremy's mom?"

Spring's mouth opened and closed. "I... You want to marry me?"

"I didn't come here tonight with the thought of proposing." He glanced around the room. "The dining room table of your friend's house is lovely, but not quite what I would have planned as the setting of a proposal. But, yes, it's a proposal, Spring. Will you marry us?"

She nodded.

They still had a lot to learn about each other, but, yes, she wanted to marry this man.

"Is that a yes?"

"Yes," she said. And then she kissed him to seal the proposal.

When the Cedar Springs City Council met again, it was the day before the engagement party for Summer Darling Spencer and Cameron Jackson. Council chambers at city hall overflowed with angry residents. Chairs had been brought in from the multipurpose room, and people stood two deep along the walls.

News of an economic development project that could reshape the region drew the attention of media well beyond the *Cedar Springs Gazette*. A couple of the television stations from both Raleigh and Fayetteville were there to report the proceedings, and the business reporters from the *Charlotte Observer*, the *News & Observer* from Raleigh and even the Norfolk, Virginia, newspapers were at the press table along with Mac Scott, the *Gazette*'s editor. The police chief had eight officers stationed around the room to quell any potential violence.

But the only truly violent outburst came from Mayor Bernadette Howell when, during the public comment period of the meeting, she was served a petition for impeachment recall.

The vote on development projects of any type or size was unanimously tabled for further study by city council, who then concluded the meeting and scuttled out of chambers under the protective escort of Cedar Springs' men and women in blue before a single reporter could approach.

"It's not over yet," Spring said as talk from residents about the meeting flowed all around them.

David sat next to her in the front row, right behind the table that had been filled with journalists.

"Nope," he said.

"For the record, I really like your proposal that incorporates our history and heritage center in it."

"The grant application you and Cecelia have is very strong."

She gave him a sidelong smile. "Thanks to the addition of some architectural renderings from a certain Charlotte-based firm that shall remain unnamed."

In the back of the city council chambers, Dr. Cecelia Jeffries confronted a man who'd shuffled in and had claimed a standing-room-only spot on the wall to watch the proceedings.

"Sweet Willie," she said.

He nodded his head toward her. "Dr. Jeffries."

In deference to the formal ambiance of the city council chambers, he'd shed the hoodie from his head. Cecelia realized it was the first time she'd seen him without the hood covering. His hair was more gray than black and he'd clearly not been associated with a razor in a few days.

"You and your folks got a victory tonight."

"Not unlike your own," she said, folding her arms across her chest and glaring at him.

"Beg pardon?"

"Why weren't you arrested with the other criminals in that burglary ring?"

"Didn't have nothing to do with it, ma'am."

She narrowed her eyes. "Why don't I believe you?"

He shrugged. "Maybe 'cause you the suspicious type." He grinned as if he'd made a joke.

Cecelia was not charmed. "There's something going on with you," she told him. "I don't know what it is, but I don't buy your act and I'm going to keep digging."

His grin grew broader. "I'm looking forward to it, Dr. Jeffries."

As the reporters either typed on laptops at the front table or moved about the council chambers interviewing city residents about the meeting and the seemingly thwarted plans for a giant retail complex in the city, David and Spring continued to talk quietly at their seats.

She laced her fingers together, stared at them for a moment, then glanced over at him. "David, I have a confession to make."

"What's that?"

"I told CeCe our secret."

"I know."

She punched him in the arm.

"Ow!" He rubbed his arm where she'd hit him. "That hurt."

"It was supposed to. I work out just about every day at my sister's gym. And how did you know?"

"The other day she winked at me and said, 'Welcome to the family, honey boy.'"

Spring laughed. "She is like a fourth sister to me."

He lifted her left hand and ran a finger along her ring finger, which remained bare of an engagement ring. "Are you sure you want to keep us just between us?"

She nodded. "For now. This is Summer's time. I don't want our news to overshadow her engagement party. She's already stressed about it. It's turned into an incredibly huge to-do. Cameron threatened to snatch her and go to Hilton Head or Savannah for a justice of the peace service and honeymoon on Tybee Island."

"And deny your mother her country club wedding and social event?"

Spring shook her head. "I feel bad for Summer and Cam. Lovie is delighted to have a wedding to plan, flowers to order, menus to see to and whatnot. And Cameron's mother is just as bad as she is. Between the two of them, this engagement party is likely to rival the actual wedding next year."

He smiled at her, an indulgent and loving smile that made Spring's insides tumble.

"That's what moms do," he said. "Indulge their kids. I know one who gave her son a teddy bear as big as he is."

Spring laughed out loud. "Something tells me we're going to end up outfitting a teddy bear for a tuxedo."

"Probably," he said.

More than 125 people milled through the formal garden at The Compound, Lovie Darling's large home.

Lovie and Carol had gone all out for the engagement party of their daughter and son. They were both dressed in identical summer suits with lace insets, Lovie's suit peach colored and Carol's in honey yellow.

Guests nibbled on finger foods, including

miniature stuffed mushrooms, assorted bruschetta and spinach-and-goat-cheese tartlets.

Autumn Darling snagged a fat shrimp from Winter's plate and chomped on it.

"You can put the coach in a dress, but you can't make her a lady," Winter said, moving her small plate out of her sister's reach.

"Back at ya," Autumn said.

She, Winter and Spring, all dressed in feminine summer shifts and heels, stood together near an arbor that, like all the garden's shrubbery and the tent's support beams, had tiny white fairy lights twinkling. The garden, always beautiful under the care of Lovie and her landscapers, was enchanting this evening. The sisters surveyed the crowd of friends and city movers and shakers and watched their sister and soon-to-be brother-in-law mingle with their well-wishers.

"By the time people finish with the appetizers, they'll be full," Autumn noted. "Do they know that Lovie has carving stations and enough food to feed half the city?"

"They're called hors d'oeuvres," Spring said.

"Thank you, Dr. Magnolia Supper Club," Winter intoned.

Autumn groaned. "Please, guys. Let's not have *that* fight tonight." She nudged Spring. "Who is that over there talking to David?"

Three pairs of blue eyes focused in on a tall

man with shaggy hair who threw his head back and laughed at whatever David had just said. He looked to be in his late twenties or early thirties and had a casual air about him that differed from the men in suits all around him. Although he wore a suit jacket, he seemed to have just a T-shirt on underneath it.

"My, my," Autumn said. "Is he one of David's architects?"

Spring shrugged. "I don't know."

"He is a looker," Winter said. "And tall, too, just the way I like them."

"I called dibs," Autumn protested.

Spring rolled her eyes at her sisters. "I'm going to go mingle. Why don't you two do the same instead of acting like you're thirteen?"

As she started to head off toward David, a tinkling of silver on crystal drew the guests' attention to a portable microphone near the arbor.

"May I have your attention, please," Cameron said. As the guests quieted down and turned his way, Spring reached David. She slipped her hand in his.

"Your mom knows how to throw a party," he said.

"That's what she majored in in college, being a gracious Southern hostess. She graduated summa cum laude in it."

He smiled. "They make a nice couple," he

said, nodding toward Cameron and Summer, who stood beaming together as Cam talked.

"They do," Summer said. "And so do we."

At the arbor, Cameron was asking their mothers to come forward.

Summer hugged Lovie, and Cameron kissed Carol on the cheek.

"We love you both very, very much," Summer said, her voice catching. "Thank you for this beautiful party."

Lovie dabbed at her eyes, and Summer pressed a small hankie into her mother's hands.

"Isn't that your minister?" David asked Spring. "What's he doing up there?"

Spring's eyes widened as she peered at Summer and then toward her other sisters, whose expressions told her they seemed to be coming to the same conclusion as she had.

"Oh my." Spring took an involuntarily step forward, taking David with her. "No, she didn't do what I think she's doing."

Summer and Cameron clasped hands and faced the Reverend Dr. Graham, pastor of First Memorial Church of Cedar Springs.

"Dearly beloved," he said. "We are gathered here today..."

Gasps rolled across Lovie Darling's garden as the two hostesses and all of the engagement party guests realized just what was happening right before their eyes. Then applause and laughter broke out. Autumn let loose with a catcall whistle that drew chuckles.

"Summer Elaine Darling, what are you doing?" Lovie asked, her voice quavering between delight and dismay.

"Exactly what you think I'm doing, Mom."

That comment earned more laughter from the impromptu wedding guests.

"Now that everyone is settled down," Reverend Graham said after a moment, "shall we continue?"

As Cameron and Summer exchanged vows under the flower-covered arbor, David and Spring gazed into each other's eyes.

"For always?" David asked her.

"For forever," Spring said.

And then he kissed her.

* * * * *

Dear Reader,

Thank you for visiting Cedar Springs with me. It's a fictional small city in North Carolina, but it feels real to me. Through the years, readers have asked how long I've lived in Carolina. The answer is never. It's a Southern state that resonates with me. I was born in Pennsylvania and have lived there and in Ohio, and now for many years Virginia has been home. But something about North Carolina draws me. So I hope you enjoy visiting as much as I enjoy writing about it.

In this, my second Cedar Springs novel for Love Inspired, I explored the concepts of single parenthood and second chances. As the eldest of the four Darling sisters, Spring believed she was responsible for setting an example for her sisters. That theme frequently plays out in real life among adult children and their younger siblings. But as Spring discovered when she fell in love with architect-consultant David Camden, you have to let go and let God have His way in your life, whether it is following a call to a ministry, being a witness or a community volunteer or finding a mate.

I love hearing from readers and welcome your comments. I can be reached at Love

Inspired Books, 233 Broadway, New York, NY 10279 USA.

Until we meet again in the pages of an inspiring novel, may God's richest blessings be yours.

Joy and peace to you,

LARGER-PRINT BOOKS!

GET 2 FREE
LARGER-PRINT NOVELS
PLUS 2 FREE
MYSTERY GIFTS

Love Inspired
SUSPENSE
RIVETING INSPIRATIONAL ROMANCE

Larger-print novels are now available...